D1524986

UNREASONABLE
FORCE

KENNETH EADE

Times Square Publishing
Copyright 2015 Kenneth Eade

ISBN: 978-1514-87000-6

For Gordon

"Injustice anywhere is a threat to justice everywhere."

-Martin Luther King

PROLOGUE

Two boys walked down the alley behind Vanowen Street, still caught up in the action of "Mortal Kombat," which they had just watched at the Topanga Theater. All pent up from the excitement, William kicked a can and it ricocheted off a fence, just missed a cat, and landed back in the middle of the alley. The heat from the summer's day lingered like a thick blanket in the atmosphere and the moon illuminated the otherwise dimly lit back street and its assortment of plastic and zinc-coated metal trash cans. Vanowen was TJ's street, and it would be easier to sneak in through the back door than to have to ring the front doorbell to get in. He knew his mom would be pissed. It was getting late and he was so excited about the film that he had forgotten to phone her before they left the theater.

"That movie was awesome!" said William, who flipped around and shot a kick at TJ, like a kickboxer in one of the scenes of the film, then with a *kiai* screech, jumped into a boxer's stance, jabbing left, right, right, left.

"Hey! Watch it!"

"Whatsa matter? You too chicken to fight?"

"No, really, man. The movie was great, but that's not somethin' you wanna be doin' in a dark alley."

"What do you mean?" asked William.

"Shit, now you went and done it!" exclaimed TJ.

"What did I do?"

"See that helicopter up there?" TJ pointed to a copter buzzing in the distance.

"Yeah, so?"

"Man, don't you know anything? He's watchin' us."

"That's bull."

"Yeah?"

"Yeah."

"Okay, smarty pants. You wanna race me to my house?"

"What for?"

"I'm gonna prove something to you."

"Yeah, right."

"Right, like it's against the law to run."

"You're full of it. It's not against the law to run."

"Yes it is. Especially for us. Ready?"

"Yeah."

William bent his right knee, in ready position, and put his knuckles on the pavement, like an Olympic runner in a sprinter's stance, while TJ did the same.

"Set."

"Go!"

The boys took off, running as fast as they could. TJ's house at the end of the alley was the finish line. TJ was sucking in and blowing out air in rhythm to his footfalls. The soles of TJ's shoes burned the bottom of his feet as he began to gain on William, but William's long legs proved the advantage as he passed TJ's backyard gate first, and jumped in the air, holding both his arms high, like a football player who had just scored a touchdown.

"I won! I won!" he yelled.

"Keep it down!" said TJ, hands on his knees, panting.

Suddenly, out of the darkness, a black and white LAPD police car screeched into the alley and came to an abrupt halt. Then it turned from night to day as the entire alley, including TJ's backyard, was illuminated by the searchlight from the overhead helicopter. It had all the trimmings of a military exercise.

Two LAPD officers jumped out of the cruiser, perched atop of the roof of the police car, pointed their guns at the boys and shouted, "Hands on your heads!" The boys' fear paled in comparison to the cops' aggression.

"Told you, man!" said TJ, putting his hands on his head.

"What the hell!" said William, putting his hands on his head, his legs shaking.

"On your knees, now!" shouted one of the officers.

The boys dropped to their knees, ignoring the pain of the asphalt grinding into their skin.

They saw the silhouette of an approaching officer, which was eclipsed by a blinding light from his baton flashlight, fixed directly at their eyes.

"That hurts!" said William.

"Shut up!" said the officer.

They didn't even see the other cop approach. He snuck up on them from behind like an alley cat after a mouse and slapped their wrists in handcuffs.

"Man, what's this about? We didn't do anything!" William protested, as the Officer picked him off the ground by the collar and slammed his body against the police car.

"I told you to shut up. You been stealin'?" he asked as he patted William down.

"No."

"Do you realize you could have been shot?"

"Shot?" William recoiled in fear. He turned to face the Officer, who slammed him back into the car. He felt like crying, but he was a man and he knew that a man had to be brave, so he forged an expression of hardened steel.

"Your buddy knows you did wrong. Look, he's pissed his pants."

William looked over at TJ, who was also against the car, being searched, his head bent in shame.

"You got any drugs?" asked the Officer.

"No, I don't do drugs."

"Don't mouth off. I'm asking you a question," the officer said, as he emptied William's pockets.

"No, I don't have any drugs."

"I found a weapon!" he called to his fellow officer.

"That's no weapon. It's my pocket knife."

The officer slipped William's Swiss Army Knife into his shirt pocket.

"My dad gave me that."

"He should have known better," said the cop, his smiling eyes betraying the stern look on his face as he pocketed the knife.

CHAPTER ONE

William Thomas was the designated driver that night. It was a great playoff game, and the best part was that the Dodgers had smeared the Cardinals in the bottom of the eighth. The smell of hot dogs and beer lingered in the corridor, which was filled with exiting spectators in a slow crawl race to get to their cars. William's buddies high-fived everyone from the patrons to the janitors on their way out of the stadium and, once they hit the open air, they waved the Dodger towels, that had been given to all at the beginning of the game, like cheerleaders at a high school football game.

"What a game!" yelled TJ, who raised his arms, sucked in his gut, pushed out his chest and strutted about in a victory dance.

"I gotta pee," said Fenton.

"Man, why didn't you pee before we left the stadium? William asked.

"Excuse me, Mr. Designated Driver. But I didn't have to pee then." Fenton laughed and slapped William on the back. TJ joined him on the other side, and the two of them started singing 'Take Me Out to the Ball Game,' as they staggered along, dragging William with them in a serpentine path through the huge parking lot, whose exit lanes had already filled with a long line of brake lights.

"Man, you guys can't sing," said William. "I'm glad I'm dropping you both off in the valley so I don't have to listen to your girly wailing all the way to Santa Barbara."

"Listen to this mofo, TJ, he lives in Santa Barbara," said Fenton, who broke away from the huddle, sucked in his ample belly, straightened up his gait, and made a snobbish face, with his nose turned up.

"Polo anyone?"

TJ almost fell to the ground laughing.

"Very funny," said William. "I have a right mind to leave you dickwads here. You can take the bus home."

"Now don't go getting all bent outta shape," said Fenton. "We was just kiddin'."

"We *were*," William corrected, which only started another round of guffaws.

TJ laughed. "I thought you *WAS* a lawyer, not an English teacher."

"Alright, alright, I'm gonna cut you guys some slack. But there's just no reason to speak like an ignorant person, when you're not one."

"There's no reason to speak like an ignorant person," mimicked Fenton, his nose high in the air, and swinging his arms like Captain Jack Sparrow.

"Wait! Wait! I gotta take a picture!" said TJ, grinning with all his teeth. He looked like Mr. Ed, the talking horse. "Smile!"

"Who couldn't smile at you and those silly ass glasses?"

"Say cheese!" TJ chimed in, and, with a goofy wink, took a picture of William with his Google glasses.

"It's too dark for that," William chuckled. "Okay, this is us," he said, gesturing to his car.

Get in," he said, and clicked open the blue Cadillac Escalade with his remote control.

"I still gotta take a piss," said Fenton as he stumbled into the back seat.

"Don't piss in my car. We'll stop on the way home."

* * *

Fenton dozed off in the back seat as William drove north on the 101 freeway. As he exited on the Burbank off ramp and turned right, Fenton popped up his head.

"I can't hold it any longer, William. Gotta go, now!"

"Just let me make it to the gas station, it's right over here."

When they pulled into the gas station, it was closed. Not exactly closed, but it was the kind where a little window was open to take your money but you couldn't come in to the store, no matter what you wanted to buy or how bad you had to pee. William spun the car around and headed for the relatively desolate area of the Sepulveda dam reservoir.

"There's no bathrooms out here," William replied. "I'm gonna head over to…"

The voice of reason was eclipsed by the more powerful voice of necessity.

"Man, the whole world's a bathroom. Just stop, and let me out now or you're gonna be sorry."

"Okay, okay," said William.

William was not as far down the boulevard as he wanted to be, but having his back seat urinated on was a less favorable option, so he brought the car to the curb right away. He had hardly pulled to a stop when Fenton was already out the door, stumbling over to the nearest bushes.

"I've gotta go too," said TJ, as he flew open the car door.

"Great!" exclaimed William, putting his hand on his head. "Well hurry up!"

"Man, what a relief!" exclaimed Fenton, as he began what seemed like an endless stream.

"You gotta turn that shit off, Bro. You're gonna flood the whole valley," said TJ.

"You know what they say?" asked Fenton.

"What?"

"If it's clear, it's beer!"

11

"Then mine has got to be beer!"

"Get back in the car, guys; hurry up!" William called out.

Just as the two staggered back, fumbling with their zippers, and entered the car, a police car pulled up behind them, its red lights on.

"Now you've done it," said William.

"Glad we've got our lawyer," said Fenton.

"Shut up and let me do the talking."

William rolled down his window as one patrolman approached the driver's side and blasted William with an assault of light, which stung his eyes. He blinked and averted his gaze.

"Look at me, sir," commanded the Officer. He seemed to be in his 30s, although William could not tell because they all looked alike in their uniforms and matching caps.

The other cop took a position to the rear of the Escalade, on the passenger's side, and shone his light into the vehicle, checking the interior.

"Got an open container!" he called out.

"License and registration," demanded the first cop, steadily training the floodlight in William's face.

"It's in the glove box. I'm going to reach over and get it, okay?"

"Just keep your hands where I can see them," said the officer.

William slowly and carefully withdrew his paperwork from the glove compartment and handed it to the policeman, who beamed the flashlight on his license, then back into William's face.

"Do you have to shine that thing in my face? I'm sensitive to bright light."

The officer didn't respond. "Step out of the car, please."

"What for?"

"Step out of the car."

As William got out of the car, he could see TJ and Fenton exiting also, their hands on their heads. They were directed to the driver's side, where the second cop put them against the car and was patting them down.

"Turn around, hands on the vehicle."

"Wait a minute, I…"

"Turn around, hands on the vehicle. I won't say it again."

William turned around and put his hands on the car. He could feel the officer's hand going up his leg. He turned his head and noticed that the cop's right hand was on his service pistol. *Great – trigger happy.*

"Turn around!"

William turned around and felt the cop reaching into his pocket, taking out his wallet. He looked to see Fenton and TJ, who were sitting on the ground, handcuffed.

"Public urination is a misdemeanor offense," said the police officer to William as he examined the contents of his wallet. "So is having an open container of alcohol."

"What open container?"

"Have you been drinking?"

"No, no. I'm the designated driver. Look officer, I'm not under the influence of alcohol."

"Did I ask you for your opinion, nigger?"

"Excuse me? Did you say '*nigger*'?"

"I didn't say anything. You said it. And isn't that what you people call each other?"

"Well, if *we people* did, that doesn't give you the right to say it."

"You ain't got any rights here, boy, 'cept the right to remain silent, and I suggest you use it."

"Why? Am I under arrest?"

"Stand with your legs together, head back, arms out straight. Close your eyes."

William complied.

"Now touch the tip of your nose with your left index finger." William touched the tip of his nose.

"I told you I'm not drunk."

"Be quiet. Now do the same with the right index finger."

William repeated the maneuver. The cop withdrew his baton and forced William's legs apart with it.

"You told me to stand with my legs together. I'll do whatever you say. Just don't hit me with that."

"Shut up. Now I want you to walk a straight line, heel to toe, until I tell you to stop and turn."

He pushed William forcefully with the baton in the back, whereupon William pushed it away with his hand.

"You don't need to keep hitting me with that stick. I'm doing everything you…"

In an instant, the cop smacked William in the knee with the baton in a rage. William felt a fire in his knee as he heard it crack, lost his balance, and fell. The cop kicked William in his balls and then his stomach, which made him heave.

"You barfed on my shoe, nigger!"

There was nothing after that, only bits and pieces. The only thing William could remember was the deafening pop as the gun went off, and the cop's partner hitting the ground like a fallen bowling pin.

CHAPTER TWO

Everything was blurry, like an impressionist painting, and as it came to focus, William recognized the bland walls and sterile furnishings of a hospital room and smelled the antiseptic atmosphere. His throat was dry. He tried to call out, but his voice wouldn't work. He heard beeping and looked to his right and saw a life signs monitor. He instinctively tried to sit up and felt the pain shoot through his ribs. His arms were frozen. Couldn't move them. He looked at his right arm and saw an IV connection. He saw the restraints a little lower down and realized that his arms had been strapped down at the wrists. He tried to move his legs, but they were immobilized as well.

A skinny female nurse came into the room. "I see you're awake."

"C-could I have some water, please?"

She rolled a tray in front of him that held a bottle of water with a straw sticking out of it. He grasped the straw with his lips and sucked the water from the straw. *Nice lady.*

"Can you please take off these restraints?" he asked. "I have to go to the bathroom."

"You'll have to ask the officer that," she said, as she left the room.

A uniformed LAPD policeman came in shortly after. He was young, with brown hair, cropped like he had just come out of Marine boot camp.

"Sir, I understand that you want me to remove your restraints, is that correct?" he asked, in a robotic tone.

William could see the repulsion in the young man's face, and he heard it in his voice. It was if his nose had been held to a pile of human feces.

"Yes, I have to go to the bathroom. How long have I been here?"

"Five days."

"Five days?" William rolled his eyes in disbelief. He struggled to sit up straight, but the shooting pain in his ribs and back, complicated by the weakness and malaise forced him to slump back down.

"Is the policeman…?"

"Dead? Yes, he is."

William hung his head. He didn't know the man but he felt sorry for him. He was probably a husband and a father. He thought of his own kids. *How one tragedy affects so many others.*

"I can't remove your restraints, sir. That's up to the detective. He's on his way."

"What am I supposed to do?"

"Use the bedpan." The cop turned and walked out.

* * *

Detective Daniel Salerno was an Italian American transplant from New York. He had known blacks from growing up in the city, and he didn't care much for them. They were lazy, had chips on their shoulders, and thought the world owed them a free ride. And this one was a cop killer. He vowed to do whatever he could to make sure that he would see him executed. The young uniformed policeman stood next to him proudly as he interviewed William.

"William Thomas?"

"Yes."

"I'm Detective Salerno from the Los Angeles Police Department. This is Officer Pike. You are under arrest for the murder of Officer David Shermer."

William couldn't believe what he was hearing. It was like he was in the middle of a nightmare over which he had no control.

"Murder?" he choked. "No, no, no…"

Salerno read from a card in his hand. "This interview pertains to criminal misconduct," he read in a monotone, computer-like voice. "Therefore, I am going to advise you of your Miranda rights. You have the right to remain silent. Do you understand?"

"I know that."

"Do you understand?"

"Yes."

"Anything you say may be used against you in court. Do you understand?"

"Yes."

"You have the right to the presence of an attorney before and during any questioning. Do you understand?"

"I want to call my attorney, now."

Salerno glared at William.

"Please let me finish the admonition; then you can call your attorney. You have the right to the presence of an attorney before and during any questioning. Do you understand?"

"Yes."

"If you cannot afford an attorney, one will be appointed for you, free of charge, before any questioning, if you want. Do you understand?"

"I understand."

"Do you want to talk about what happened?"

"Not to you. I want my lawyer."

Salerno turned to leave.

"Wait!"

"Yes?" He pivoted at the doorway.

"Can I see my wife?"

"This hospital is not equipped to handle prisoners. When your doctor OKs your transfer to County Jail, she can visit you per the visitor's schedule."

Salerno was gone. William's head was spinning so fast, he had forgotten to ask about the restraints. He tried to move his arms as he called out, "What about these restraints?"

The question was either not heard or it fell on deaf ears.

CHAPTER THREE

Brent Marks didn't take many criminal defense cases these days, especially from Los Angeles, but when he got the call from William Thomas, he made an exception and decided to consider it. William was a colleague that Brent had met during a securities fraud case. Ten years his junior, William had put up a great fight, all the way through the trial. He was a good lawyer, and through the years they had become friends.

The ride from Santa Barbara to the San Fernando Valley was not so bad in the afternoon, but it would be hell coming back, up until about 8 o'clock. As he watched the headlights of the cars inching their way toward him in slow motion on the northbound side of the 101 freeway, he thought of how he had commuted to law school in downtown L.A. for three years, and pondered how people wasted so much of their lives driving two or three hours to work and two or three hours back, day after day, year after year. It made him feel especially grateful that he lived in Santa Barbara, and only five minutes away from his office. He pulled into Olive View Medical Center in Sylmar. A few minutes later he was meeting with his old friend and potential new client.

Brent showed his bar card and ID to the officer on guard and told him that he needed to have a confidential discussion with his client. Then he walked in.

"William?"

The man in the hospital bed was not the big, strong, strapping man with the million dollar smile whom Brent had always known. This was a man in pieces.

"Brent, thank you so much for coming."

"You look pretty busted up here, William."

"Yeah. Six broken ribs, a broken knee…"

"And your face looks like you took on Mike Tyson, Evander Holyfield and Floyd Merriweather all at the same time."

"I'm in deep shit, man."

"That's why I'm here. Tell me what happened."

The TV droned in the background. *Eyewitness News has just learned that a video of last week's shooting of a Metro Division LAPD officer has been released to You Tube, where it has already received over 3 million hits...*

"Brent, listen!"

Brent grabbed the remote control and turned up the volume. The video was disjointed, about 30 seconds long, and looked like it had been pieced together. It showed William wrestling on the ground with a uniformed police officer.

"Where did this video come from?" Brent asked.

"I don't know. TJ had on Google glasses. Maybe he took it."

"That would explain why it's so short."

The name of the suspect, a black man who appears to be in his thirties, is being withheld by police pending investigation...

"Listen to them, Brent. If you're black, you'll always be referred to as a 'black man,' never just a 'man.' If there's no black man involved, they never say 'a white man' or 'two white men.' They just say 'two men.'"

"It's Jim Crow, all over again."

"Brent, that policeman stopped me for *nothing*. And even after he stopped me, he should have seen who I *was*. But he didn't see a human being. He didn't see a man with hopes and dreams, with disappointments and accomplishments. All he saw in front of him was just *another nigger*."

Brent knew that William's case emphasized the black and white line that had been drawn between police and people of color in the United States. Police organizations followed a paramilitary structure and protocol, and their members had all been trained in a military fashion. Through years of desensitization, the public had come to accept the "us" or "them" mentality, and had looked the other way to violence on its own soil in the name of "safety," especially after the war on terror was announced after September 11, 2001. Just as the military in war objectify and dehumanize the enemy, the enemy in the war on the streets of America had a face, and it was not white.

William recounted events that transpired upon leaving the stadium, up until the point when he was on the ground.

"After that, it's a blank."

"Whose hand was the gun in when it went off?"

"I don't know."

"Who squeezed the trigger?"

"I don't know."

"'I don't know' doesn't set very well for your defense, William."

"That's just it. I don't know who shot the gun – him or me – it just went off. I don't remember anything. I'm no expert, Brent, but it doesn't look too good for me, does it?"

"No, it doesn't."

"Will you take my case?"

"Yes, but we have to formulate some kind of theory of defense."

"Brent?"

"Yes?"

"You're the criminal defense guy, not me. Can it be self-defense when you shoot someone else – not the guy you were defending yourself from?"

"That's something I don't know, William. I have to find out."

CHAPTER FOUR

Los Angeles Police Department Chief Charles Penwald addressed a crowd of reporters inside the press room in the sleek glass and concrete headquarters of the LAPD. In back of him was a blue curtain, imprinted with LAPD logos, which could have served as a backdrop for some red carpet Hollywood event.

"We have a suspect in custody in the shooting of Metro Division Police Officer David Shermer," he read from a prepared statement, matter-of-factly.

"As with all officer-involved shootings, LAPD Specialized Force Investigation Division responded to preserve and collect evidence, and interview witnesses to the shooting.

"As you know, portions of this incident were caught on video. I have reviewed the video, and it is clear to me that the other officer's gun was grabbed by the suspect, who discharged the weapon, fatally injuring Officer Shermer."

That should make it easy to pick a jury, thought Brent.

"Photos of the officer's service weapon appear on my right. As you can see, the slide is partially engaged and a second round has been partially ejected and has fouled the firing chamber. This is indicative of force being used on the weapon.

"We will, of course, be conducting an extensive investigation…"

Of course.

"Can you identify the suspect?" asked a female reporter from the second row of the packed room.

"We cannot identify the suspect at this time, as our investigation is continuing. But we have made an arrest and the District Attorney will announce the identity of the suspect at the appropriate time."

"Don't you think this shooting indicates a racist pattern, and are you covering that issue in your investigation?" asked a male voice from the background.

"It is true that the suspect is African American, but I can assure you that the Los Angeles Police Department selects and trains its officers carefully and we do not tolerate racial inequality in any respect."

Brent picked up the remote control and switched off the television in his living room. He rarely watched it, but wanted to keep up to date on the latest that was happening on the investigation, which seemed to be progressing at lightning speed. His cat, Calico, jumped up on the couch with him and started to purr.

"I know what you want," said Brent, as he reached for the bag of cat treats on the coffee table. Calico began a "catlong rub" from whiskers to tail against Brent's face, and her snaky tail tickled his nose. He opened the bag, which emanated the pungent smell of dried fish.

"Yeesh!"

Once Brent had fetched the treat out of the bag and given it to the cat, her display of affection immediately ceased and she jumped off the couch. She knew the rule was only one treat at a time.

Brent's cell phone rang. The only thing he liked less than talking on the phone was the ridiculous electronic musical ringers. He didn't have the time or the patience to sit with his phone and go through what seemed like hundreds of tunes to pick the perfect ringer, so he opted for the default one. *Why can't they just make a phone that rings like a phone?*

"Oh hi, Angie. I was just going to call you."

"Really? When?"

"Very funny. I'm pulling a night shift tonight."

"New case?"

"Yeah."

"What is it?"

"Have you seen the news lately?"

"Not the police shooting?"

"Yup. I'm meeting Jack in about a half an hour."

"Couldn't you do it after dinner?"

"We're working through dinner."

"I'm sure you would have liked it at my place better."

"I always do."

When Brent walked into Sonny's Bar and Grill on State Street in downtown Santa Barbara, he knew it was the worst place to have a meeting on a Friday night. The bar was packed with partiers, all set to leave their inhibitions (and their sobriety) behind. It smelled like stale beer and wet wood, and the ample sound system belted out AC/DC screaming "Dirty Deeds Done Dirt Cheap."

The only thing out of place at the bar was Jack Ruder. He sat among the after-work crowd who were in jeans or various other stages of undress, oblivious to the fact that he was an alien. Even the executives straight out of the boardrooms and the banks had the sense to chuck their ties and leave their jackets in the car. But there was Jack, in a crisp suit that looked like he had just taken it from the dry cleaners. He always had that stiff, cop-type look, even when he had a beer in his hand. Brent supposed it came from a lifetime career with the FBI before he retired. Now Jack spent his working days (and a great deal of his nights) as a private eye.

"Hey Jack, great place for a meeting!" yelled Brent, in competition with AC/DC and a hundred voices each competing to rise above the collective volume, as he approached Jack and reached for his hand.

"Yeah, I thought we should meet in a quiet place where we could talk," Jack screamed back as he completed the shake.

"So what do you think? You want in?"

"Ex-FBI agent defends cop-killer? Why not? My reputation with local law enforcement could use a boost."

"I knew you couldn't resist this one."

Brent ordered a Corona and a burger from the bartender.

"What's first?" asked Jack.

"I'm going to talk to the buddies who were with William. You try to talk to the cop. I want to know as much as we can as soon as we can in case they don't let William out on bail."

"But he's a local attorney with no criminal history; he's not a flight risk."

"Tell that to the judge who's running for re-election on a tough on crime platform. I can't see him getting out before trial."

"There's something that doesn't make sense to me about this case already," said Jack.

"What?"

"What were two officers from Metro Division assigned to North Hollywood doing patrolling Sherman Oaks alone on a Saturday night?"

CHAPTER FIVE

Timothy Jones (or "TJ" as his friends called him) was a tech geek. A computer whiz, he handled a major portion of San Fernando Valley small business's computer needs. His home was an upscale south of Ventura Boulevard spread in Encino in a neighborhood that screamed "well to do." Upon being welcomed in by TJ's wife, a lovely slender lady with chocolate complexion, Brent looked around the place and could see that it was well equipped with every gadget imaginable. There was a bigger-than-big-screen TV in the living room with stacks of electronic boxes alongside it, including cable, TIVO, a home security system, and TV Internet. TJ's wife directed Brent to his home office, a den filled with computers and TV monitors and packed with electronic contraptions.

"Honey, this is Brent Marks, William's lawyer."

"Come on in, Brent," TJ said as he rotated his cockpit-style Recaro chair away from the larger-than-life trio of computer monitors and stood to greet Brent. He was a big man, slightly overweight, with a pleasant smile, a firm grip, and a scratchy voice.

Brent took a seat in the leather couch on the opposite wall.

"You've got a lot of toys here."

"When you're in the IT business, it's an occupational prerequisite," said TJ. "Plus they're fun to play with."

"Tell me about the video you took."

"Well, I almost forgot I had those glasses on, because I was so scared."

"Can I see them?"

"Sure," TJ said, as he picked up a pair of regular-looking brown plastic-rim glasses, with thick sides and handed them to Brent.

"I designed the frames to hide the device. If you look on the right side, you can see the mechanism."

"Where?" Brent asked as he turned the glasses around in his hands.

"Right here," said TJ, pointing to a small rectangular implement that appeared to have a clear plastic lens.

"And how do you take pictures?"

"You just wink. I'll show you."

Brent handed the glasses to TJ, who put them on, looked at Brent, and winked.

"And a video?"

"I just say, 'Okay glass, record a video.' The default videos are ten seconds long. To make them longer, I have to use the control pad."

"Which you couldn't do."

"Not with my hands cuffed. So I took a succession of ten second videos and cut all the good ones together."

"What did you do with the bad ones?"

"Oh, I still have them, but they didn't make the final cut."

"Why not?"

"They were mostly too dark, not enough light. Couldn't make out anything that was going on."

TJ put the video on the big screen and they watched it together.

"This is where William pushed the gun out of the way."

"You don't think he was trying to grab the gun away from the officer?"

"Well, maybe. Man, what would you do? That guy was going to kill him for sure. He was coked up with testosterone and pissed off that William wouldn't let him push him around with his stupid stick. All he saw was black, and I don't think that's his favorite color, if you know what I mean."

40

"I do. Tell me what you saw."

"After William pushed the stick away, that crazy cop broke his knee cap with the club and William fell. Then he jumped on him, stuck his gun in his face and said, "You're gonna die, nigger. Your momma won't even recognize you at your funeral.""

"But you didn't get that all on video?"

"Unfortunately not. I just kept telling the glass to record. There's a gap between every ten second sequence."

"Can I have a copy of all the original footage?"

"Sure."

"Did you also give the police the original?"

"No, they just asked for 'the video' so I gave them the final cut. Are you going to call us to testify?"

"If it goes to trial. Only one problem."

"What?"

"You guys were both drunk."

"Believe me, Brent. You see something like that, and it sobers you up, right quick."

CHAPTER SIX

Jack didn't get a very warm reception at the LAPD. Luckily, since he had worked for them in the old days before his FBI career, he still knew some of the old-timers who had made their way pretty high up in the department. Jack went straight to LAPD headquarters and met with Capt. Martin Tennyson, the commanding officer of the Force Investigation Division.

"Hello Marty," said Jack, as he stood in the doorway of Tennyson's office.

Tennyson blew out a stream of smoke as he sprouted a full smile of nicotine-stained teeth.

"I thought it was against the law to smoke in public buildings," said Jack.

"Not when you're the boss."
Tennyson crushed out his cigarette in a large tray cluttered with a collection of burned out

butts, the predominant object on his desk, besides the pig-shaped lighter.

"Damn it, Jack! Is it true? You're working for the lawyer who's representing the cop killer?" asked Tennyson as Jack entered the wood paneled office which brimmed with trophies and pictures of the seasoned lawman with various politicians who had come and gone through the years.

"Good to see you too, Marty."

"Hell, have a seat, Jack. It's been a long time," Tennyson said as he rose to shake Jack's hand. Jack sat down in one of the velour chairs opposite Tennyson's walnut desk.

"I don't suppose we could talk you into working for the right side?"

"I'm working for the same thing you are, Marty – to find out the truth."

"Once a cop, always a cop. You even still look like a policeman, Jack."

"I get that all the time. Can I cut to the chase?"

"Yeah, we can catch up on 20 years' lost time over a beer sometime, I hope. I can't give you anything on the Shermer case, Jack. The D.A. has it sewed up tighter than the panties of a farmer's daughter."

"I have a subpoena."

"Hell, Jack. Why don't you just get the info from the D.A.?"

"Like you said, they're not releasing anything until the arraignment."

"Okay, gimme that Goddamned subpoena, then."

Jack handed over a two-sheet piece of paper. Tennyson put on his reading glasses and looked at it as he grabbed his pack of Chesterfields from his desk and popped one out, catching it between his teeth.

"I can let you see the reports, but you can't interview Officer Albright," he said as he inserted the cigarette between his teeth.

"Did he make a statement?"

"Yeah, I'll call it up now." Tennyson picked up his marble pig-shaped lighter from the desk and lit up his cig, puffing smoke in short bursts. It was then that Jack realized that there were pigs all over his office. Statues of pigs in police garb, photos of pigs on police motorcycles, pictures of pigs putting handcuffs on bad guys, and police car models with pig heads sticking out the window.

"Pigs, Marty?"

Tennyson shrugged his shoulders and beamed.

"And I'll need copies of the autopsy report on Shermer."

"That you'll have to get from the Coroner, but I can't give you everything on this list, Jack."

"Why not?"

"It's still an active investigation."

"Look, just give me what you can and I'll let Brent Marks sort out the rest with the D.A. And there's one more thing."

Tennyson looked at Jack with impatience. "What?"

"What was a lone Metro unit assigned to NoHo doing on Burbank Boulevard in Sherman Oaks? That's not exactly a high crime area, is it?"

"Not usually, but they had an assignment nearby and stopped when they saw suspicious activity. You know all cops do that, Jack. It's either our sense of duty or our damned curiosity."

Jack left Tennyson's office with a modest stack of papers. Albright had completed his psychological briefing after the shooting, had been issued a new firearm, and was back in service. His statement was the most revealing.

The suspect became belligerent and violent during a routine examination for driving under the influence. He became combative and reached out and grabbed my baton, which I had withdrawn prior to the examination for my own safety when he had failed to follow verbal commands. I pulled the baton away from him and struck him on the knee to regain control. The suspect refused to be handcuffed, and I was forced to defend myself from his violent advances. The suspect then wrestled me to the ground and a struggle ensured. I subdued him, whereupon he reached for my pistol and withdrew it from the holster. I attempted to regain control of the pistol, but, before I could wrestle it away from his grip, he fired one round, which hit and killed Officer Shermer. He attempted to fire another round, but at that point, I was able to retrieve the weapon and render the suspect unconscious to prevent any more bloodshed.

CHAPTER SEVEN

William sat on the bunk in his cell at the Men's Central Jail and looked out through the bars confining him to the three filthy walls of his cell that probably used to be white. More bars. Trash bags. Scumbags. The smell of years upon years of collective loneliness, guilt and shame was a foul mixture of body odor, bad breath, garbage and human excrement. He covered his ears to try to shut out the combined roar of talking, screaming and toilets flushing.

Sadness and misery covered William's entire body like a heavy, dirty blanket, and the melancholy settled in his stomach like he had eaten something rotten. *Come on, William, you're gonna make it through this,* he said to himself. He had always been the one who was positive. Always saw the glass half full to the point he would annoy his friends with his optimism. But this was an all-time low that he had reached in his life. There was no bright side left to look at. All that was left was despair.

"You get used to it," said William's bunkmate, a young man whose head was covered with matted coils of dreadlocks. "I been here for nine months."

William didn't really feel like socializing, but the man seemed to be trying to be friendly, so he gave a courtesy reply, "Thanks, man."

"Besides," said the young man. "I hear you a big ass cop killer. Ain't nobody gonna mess wichu in here."

* * *

Brent flipped through the pages of the police report, looked up at Jack across his desk, and took a sip of coffee. He shook his head.

"So it was William who attacked the cop and shot Shermer."

"That's what they say. It's the word of a decorated officer against William and two drunk guys."

This gave Brent pause as he thought whether his entire case would come down to a pissing contest between three black guys and one white guy in front of an all-white jury. He kneaded the coffee cup handle with his thumb and forefinger as he thought.

"But it was a routine traffic stop."

"Lots of cops get blown away during routine traffic stops."

"Yeah, but the guy's got six broken ribs, a broken knee, and he's been in a coma for five days. Doesn't that sound like excessive force?"

"I've been on the other side of this, Brent. William's a big guy. You'd have to use a considerable amount of force to subdue him."

"Yes, but that's our whole case, isn't it? Unreasonable force is illegal. The force used has to be reasonable under the circumstances to protect the police officers and the public."

"And in this case, there was no public."

"Right. Unarmed William was the public. Drunk Fenton and TJ were the public. We're most likely going to have a jury of middle class whites. Most of them have never had a bad experience with the police. We need to spin our case so that they have to do more than just decide whether William or Albright are telling the truth."

"How do we do that?"

"We make them feel uncomfortable about the amount of force that was used by Albright during the stop. Hey, I got something interesting from TJ during the interview."

Brent handed Jack the disk with all the video footage on it.

"There's twice as much video on here than we've seen. Let's get it enhanced so we can try to see more of what really happened. And let's get an audio guy to enhance the audio track."

"No problem."

CHAPTER EIGHT

Brent hit the books to test his new theory of the case. These days "the books" didn't mean those dusty, moldy volumes of law books that lawyers used to have to schlep off the shelves and pile onto a desk in stacks. It was all done with a keyboard and a mouse now. Brent flew through the cases, skimming them on his laptop and copying the notable ones for comprehensive reading later.

The research made it clear that the doctrine of "transferred intent" meant that if you shot at one person and hit and killed a third person, you were guilty of murder. However, if you are exercising a lawful right to self-defense when you shoot at the first person, you cannot be held responsible for the death of the third party, as you have no criminal intent to kill them. That cleared up William's worry, but Brent's theory of defense called for a lot more research.

As the day wore on, Brent lost track of time and stuck to the task like a bee foraging for nectar. A welcome silence came over the office after 5 p.m., as the phones stopped ringing, his secretary Melinda stopped asking questions (which always broke his concentration), and the clicking of his keyboard didn't have to compete with any other office noises.

The cases seemed to indicate that when a police officer makes a traffic stop, he is allowed to use some degree of physical coercion to effectuate it. But the force used must be reasonable in order to effectuate an arrest, prevent escape, or to overcome resistance.

The determination of whether the force used is reasonable under the Fourth Amendment, which is intended to protect the public from unreasonable arrests and searches, requires careful attention to the facts and circumstances of each particular case, including the severity of the suspected crime at issue, whether the suspect poses an immediate threat to the safety of the officers or others, and whether he is actively resisting arrest or attempting to evade arrest by flight.

In William's case, the suspected crime of driving under the influence of alcohol was hardly one that required a great degree of force.

However, Jack did have a point in that policemen approaching unknown strangers in the middle of the night often are assaulted and even killed under the most unlikely of circumstances. Brent read on.

The 'reasonableness' of a particular use of force must be judged from the perspective of a 'reasonable officer' on the scene, rather than with the 20/20 vision of hindsight. That 'reasonable officer' is not the perfect cop, but one whose actions you would reasonably expect under any particular set of facts. As Jack noted, you also had to take into account that police officers are often forced to make split-second judgments in circumstances that are tense, uncertain, and rapidly evolving; about the amount of force that is necessary in a particular situation.

An officer's fear for his safety is a factor upon which he can reasonably rely, either for investigating further potential criminality or for containing a threat. But, an officer's use of deadly force is *only reasonable if the officer has probable cause to believe that the suspect poses a significant threat of death or serious physical injury to the officer or others.*

Hence, the D.A. would argue in Court that Officers Albright and Shermer approached

William's vehicle when they saw it sitting on the side of the road with the driver inside of it and two passengers outside of the car engaged in suspicious (and possibly illegal activity), which gave them the right to detain the occupants and investigate.

During the investigation, Officer Albright observed that the two occupants were intoxicated and instructed William to exit the car and perform some routine tests to determine if he was under the influence of alcohol. He became combative and tried to grab Officer Albright's baton. William continued to act violently, making Officer Albright fear for his safety, so he attempted to subdue him. During this process, there was a struggle over Officer Albright's gun. William seized it, fired the fatal shot, and attempted to fire another shot when Albright wrestled it away.

Brent reached for a glass of water, as he realized he was parched. Not only that, his stomach was growling. Continuing to research at this time without energy would be futile. The silence was broken by a knock on the office door.

Brent opened the door to the lovely sight of Angela Wollard.

"Angie, what a great surprise!"

"I came to invite you to a picnic," she said, as she flew her arms around him and kissed him on the neck. The warmth of her body radiated through his as she squeezed.

"I thought picnics were for afternoons. It's already…" He looked at his watch "…seven o'clock."

"This picnic's in my dining room," she said, brushing her lovely light brown locks from her springtime green eyes. How could this invitation be refused?

"I can't think of a better place. I'd be delighted."

CHAPTER NINE

Judge Malcom Leonard was a tough-on-crime judge, which meant that Brent could expect him not to exhibit any leniency toward William at his arraignment. The only real order of business at an arraignment was to plead guilty or not guilty to the charge. However, it was also the first opportunity to seek William's release on bail. Brent met with William in the holding cells behind Department 100 in the Van Nuys West Courthouse before court.

"Brent, you've got to get me out of here." William looked at Brent with wide-eyed hope.

"Sorry to tell you this, William, but I don't think the chances of getting you out before trial are very good."

"But my family's here. My career is here. How could they think I would run under those circumstances?"

"Your lack of a criminal record, the likelihood that you will appear at your trial, and all your appearances are all factors the judge will consider."

"Then why do you think my chances aren't good?"

"One of the other factors is the seriousness of the offense. Now, a judge can't set an excessive bail no matter what the offense, but he can deny bail in a capital murder case."

"I know it's not up to you. Just do your best to get me out. The guards aren't too nice to accused cop killers in County."

"Don't worry, William; I will. I'll see you in there."

Brent got up and turned to leave.

"And Brent?"

"Yes?"

"In case I don't get out, could you please keep an eye on Sarah and the kids for me?"

"Of course, William."

Brent took advantage of the fact that he arrived early, before the hustle and bustle of arraignment court had begun, to meet with the Assistant District Attorney on William's case. She was a plain-looking, mousy-haired 30-something in a classic business suit, with a wire cart (like a shopping cart) full of case files. Brent summoned up all his charm, even though he felt it would be wasted on her, and took his best shot before the judge took the bench, approaching the busy woman in the midst of shuffling her papers.

"Excuse me, Ms.?"

"Heartland; Jean Heartland. Pleased to meet you, Mr.?"

"Brent Marks. I've got the Thomas case."

"My most interesting one. Murder of a police officer."

"Yes, well, that is the accusation. I wanted to discuss the release of the defendant."

"Well, we're going to ask for no bail."

"I was hoping for an O.R." This meant a release on William's own recognizance, a request she greeted with an "Are you kidding?" smile.

"That would, for sure, get me fired. My boss would like to win the next election for District Attorney."

"Will you stipulate to a reasonable bail?"

"Ordinarily I would ask what you thought was reasonable; but in this case, I've been instructed not to make any agreements, and just put it before the court."

"And ask for no bail."

"Right."

Judge Leonard took the bench half an hour late. He looked impatiently through his wire-rimmed glasses at the gallery full of people of all walks of life: the front row of attorneys (whose cases would be called first, so they could move on to the next courtroom) and the jury box (loaded with prisoners; most of them who had, most likely, been here many times before). For Leonard, it was an endless stream of scumbags pleading guilty and receiving their punishment, or pretending they weren't guilty and going on to try to find a better deal. He looked down at his overloaded calendar and called the first case.

"The Court calls the case of People v. Thomas. Counsel, please state your appearances."

"Good morning, Your Honor: Jean Heartland for the people."

"Good morning, Your Honor: Brent Marks, appearing with defendant William Thomas, who is present in custody, who waives a reading of his rights."

William stood up in the jury box where all the defendants in custody were held, handcuffed and sporting ankle chains.

"Good morning to you both. Mr. Marks, to the charge of capital murder, how does your client plead?"

"Not guilty, Your Honor."

"Does your client waive time for trial, Mr. Marks?"

"That depends on the pre-trial release terms, your Honor."

"Your Honor, the People in this case request that bail not be set. This is a serious charge involving the murder of a police officer engaged in his official duties."

"It is a serious charge. Mr. Marks?"

"Your Honor, the defendant is a respected attorney in Santa Barbara County with no prior criminal record. He has a wife and two small children, and extended family in the area. He poses no flight risk in this case."

Judge Leonard's forehead wrinkled. He flipped through the pages of the file, pretending to give the request serious consideration. But, in reality, he had already decided.

"Mr. Marks, the defendant is charged with the murder of a police officer: a crime from which, if convicted, he could be punished by death. The Court has no choice in this matter but to deny bail."

William hung his head down, depressed and discouraged.

CHAPTER TEN

Brent knew that it would be difficult to have William examined by a psychiatrist while he was in custody, but the primary weakness in their case had to be addressed. So long as William didn't remember anything about the crucial moment when the shot was fired, he could not be called upon to testify. While it was true that he couldn't be forced to testify, if he remained silent, the jury would always be wondering why he didn't explain his side of the story, and that would tend to sway them against him. It was human nature.

Brent contacted Dr. Lucille Reading, a psychiatrist with whom he had worked in the past. It would be easier to get her into the jail to interview William at any time because she was also a lawyer. Reading agreed to an evaluation interview with William to determine his condition for a treatment plan, if any.

* * *

The Men's Central Jail in downtown Los Angeles was mainly a holding facility for people awaiting their trials, but it also held convicts who were serving out their sentences there instead of in prison. It was ancient, built in 1963 and renovated in the 70's, and was considered to be a high security prison. William was sitting in his cell when the Guard arrived, which caused a ruckus among the inmates, who were shouting and waving their arms outside the bars of their cells.

"Shut up!" screamed the Guard. "Anyone who doesn't is going in the hole!

"Thomas, you've got a visitor," the guard said as he unlocked the door of William's cell.

As the guard escorted William through the cell block, he could hear the collective screams of, "Cop killer! Cop killer!" While it gave William a certain status on the inside, the guard was thinking the same thing the inmates were chanting, but with contempt toward him.

The guard led William into a locked corridor, filled with inmates, each sitting on small steel stools in cubicles in front of reinforced glass windows. He sat down on the stool assigned to him and almost cried when he saw the face of his wife, Sarah. As he picked up the black telephone to his right, he realized that this was the first time he had seen her smile since he had been arrested.

Sarah brushed her golden hair from her porcelain face and picked up the phone. William drank in her beauty and imagined her sweet smell, which was blocked by the thick pane of glass.

"Sarah, I'm so glad you came."

"I don't like seeing you in this place, but it's so hard not seeing you at all."

Eyes of pale turquoise pools brimmed with sadness, which Sarah tried to hide behind a genuine smile. William put his hand against the glass and Sarah mirrored the gesture.

"How are Danny and Sissy doing?"

"They're fine. Danny just lost his first tooth. Sissy's learning how to read."

Sarah held out her hand to reveal a small tooth in its palm, and William choked back tears. He hadn't been away for that long and yet he had already missed so much.

"What did you tell them?"

"That Daddy had to be away for a while, but that he would be coming home soon. Sissy made a picture for you."

Sarah held up a crayoned masterpiece with four stick figures in front of a house and a bright yellow smiling sun in the background. The girl stick figure was holding the father's hand.

"It's beautiful. Could you send it to me by mail? I'd like to put it up on my wall."

"Of course, William. Brent told me they denied you bail."

"Yeah. But he's working really hard on my case."

"He's a good lawyer, William. I know he'll get you out of here."

"Visiting time is up, Thomas," called a sentry at the end of the corridor. After a little taste of heaven, William was sent back into the depths of his living hell.

* * *

The cop jumped on top of William. It was hard to breathe. He pointed his gun right at his face. "I'm gonna kill you, nigger," the cop said. William panicked and grabbed the gun.

"You think you're tough shit, don't you, cop killer?"

William felt the restriction around his neck, cutting off his air supply. He gasped for air, and opened his eyes to face his attacker, the inmate in green scrubs, the new neighbor who shared his cell. The burn of adrenalin radiating out from his chest gave him a surge of strength. He wrenched free his fist and jammed it into his attacker's nose, which flowed blood like a faucet as he threw the man off his bed.

"You'll be sorry for this," said the prisoner, holding his nose with his bloody hands.

The cell block reacted like a bunch of caged apes in a zoo. Three guards ran to the cell, opened it, searched and handcuffed William, and took him out.

"You're going in the hole," one of them said.

CHAPTER ELEVEN

Jack Ruder busied himself interviewing the officers who arrived on the scene that night. As hard as he tried, it was virtually impossible to break their code of silence. All six of them placed William as the aggressor; a revelation that Jack thought very odd, due to the fact that William was unconscious almost immediately upon their arrival. His fingerprints (and Albright's) were all over the gun, and the report of the official LAPD investigation showed that the gun had been tampered with. All of these facts pointed to William, who had no memory to contest them, and his corroborating witnesses were both drunk at the time.

Dr. Reading was having about the same luck with William, herself. Her time was limited and it was difficult working with him because it was impossible for him to relax, and during the time he spent in solitary confinement, he was unavailable to her. However, she was able to diagnose William as suffering from post-traumatic stress disorder, and surmised the PTSD was what was causing the memory loss. And that was more than a hunch. Her diagnosis was supported by samples of William's blood made available to her by the county hospital.

William didn't have much respect for psychology, but Dr. Reading was intelligent and easy to talk to. She was also a medical doctor and an attorney, and had a calm manner about her. She was about 45 years old, but could have passed for ten years younger. She wasn't unpleasant to look at either, with her long auburn hair and forest green eyes.

"William, these flashbacks – do you have any recall of details from them?"

"Not really. They're always just bits and pieces, and I only see them when I'm asleep."

"I'd like to try something called exposure therapy. It might help you organize those bits and pieces into real memories and, at the same time, lessen the nightmares."

"Whatever works, Doc."

"Alright. As they say, there's no time to begin like the present . I'm going to show you a series of photos, and I want you to tell me the first thing that comes to your mind."

"Not inkblots…"

"Not at all."

Dr. Reading held up the first photo, a crime scene photograph of Officer Shermer's dead body.

"That's the second cop. The one who got shot."

"Good, William. And this one?"

"The first cop. Albright."

Reading continued to flash police photographs that had been taken of the scene: the abandoned police car with its flashing lights still on; William's car, abandoned.

"It's no use, Doc. Nothing's coming back."

"This takes time, William."

"That's the ironic thing about time, Doc. On the one hand, we don't have much of it; but it's all I have in here."

* * *

It was Monday, Brent's least favorite day of the week and also the day for William's preliminary hearing. Brent had spent the weekend preparing, even though it would mainly be a show that the prosecution put on. The only question to be decided was whether the judge found that the facts presented would "lend a man of ordinary care and prudence to believe and conscientiously lead to an honest and strong suspicion that the person accused is guilty of a crime." It was a very low bar for the D.A. to reach, and, if the prosecution prevailed at the preliminary hearing, as it usually did, William would be held to answer for the murder of Officer Shermer at trial.

The hearing was to be held in Judge John Hinman's department and, although Hinman would not be the trial judge, Brent would have the chance to meet, for the first time, the Deputy D.A. who would be prosecuting the case. His name was Benjamin Taylor, a veteran prosecutor with an undefeated record as well as political aspirations to take over his boss's position as District Attorney of Los Angeles County. Brent made it to the courtroom on time, as he had met with William in the holding cell to prepare him for the hearing. He had hoped to meet Taylor, but he was nowhere in sight.

74

Even as the courtroom filled up, Taylor was still absent. Brent, searching for an explanation, exited into the corridor and there he found His Majesty, holding his own court with a gaggle of reporters. An adept politician, he stood perfectly comfortably among them in his blue-grey two piece suit with cobalt blue shirt and royal blue tie. Not one of his light brown hairs was out of place as he played to the video cameras.

"We predict that this case will go to trial," Taylor was pontificating. *Not that there was any other outcome to be expected.* "And that it will send a strong message to criminals everywhere that law and order is alive and well in Los Angeles County."

Brent ventured into the fray just as a woman reporter asked, "What about allegations of police brutality in this case?"

"I can answer that," said Brent, taking the spotlight away from Taylor. He usually didn't like to address reporters, but he didn't care for Taylor's roundabout way of poisoning the jury pool, even if it was not, perhaps, his primary intention.

"Brent Marks, attorney for the defense," Brent announced to Taylor, with an outstretched hand, and was swallowed up by the mob of reporters. Taylor shook Brent's hand very firmly and flashed a phony smile of bleached white teeth amid the popping flashes. Taylor stole the limelight back with another political pronouncement of law and order.

"It seems that, whenever there is an unfortunate violent incident such as this, involving a police officer, the defense tries to hide behind the veil of police brutality. However, it is the policy of my office not to discuss the merits of a case before trial."

Oh really? Then what have you been doing out here for God knows how long?

Brent fired back, "The young lady had a very pertinent question. This entire case rests on the question of whether the police officer used unreasonable force in detaining my client. We contend that the amount of force was excessive under the circumstances, and that the officer's actions in detaining my client were illegal."

This stirred up the journalists, who always enjoyed a good dose of controversy to serve with their entertainment.

"What about that, Mr. Taylor?" asked a seasoned correspondent from the local ABC news, coming at him hotly with her microphone. He regarded it as if it were a weapon and signaled that the impromptu press conference was over.

"We will have comments after the hearing," said Taylor. "I'm confident that we will prevail at the preliminary hearing and that Mr. Thomas will be held to answer for this heinous crime against society." Taylor waved, shot a concealed, dirty glare at Brent, and opened the door to the courtroom.

"So am I," said Brent, sparking a rumble of questions from the reporters. "The defendant is almost always held to answer in a preliminary hearing, because the burden of proof is so low. It's pretty much a show for the prosecution."

Once inside, Taylor furiously set his briefcase on the counsel table and shot an accusatory finger at Brent.

"Another incident like that and I will have no resort but to report you to the Bar."

"I could say the same for you," answered Brent. "But let's not get off on the wrong foot."

Taylor didn't answer Brent's offer to push the reset button. Instead, he removed his files and outlines from his briefcase and methodically placed them on the counsel table. The first battle was on.

CHAPTER TWELVE

Judge Jonathan Hinman traditionally called all the attorneys into his chambers for a conference before every preliminary hearing. He had quite a full calendar, but William's case was given priority not because the judge particularly cared to give the prosecution's star first string player special treatment, but he knew that the case was a hot potato and he wanted to pass it out of his courtroom as quickly as possible. He also needed to determine how much time to set aside for the hearing so he could shuffle around the other cases on his calendar and try to accommodate everybody. Anything he wouldn't have the time to handle or that couldn't be settled or continued would be sent to another department. The Judge reviewed the file, then looked at Brent and Taylor over the rims of his reading glasses. Then, removing them, he asked in his calculated baritone voice, "Ben, what's the offer on this case?"

"There is none, Your Honor."

The Judge's salt and pepper eyebrows furrowed. "I've read the file. Do you really think you have a slam dunk here?"

"Yes we do, Your Honor."

"So you want to take this to trial?"

"Yes, Your Honor."

"What about you, Mr. Marks? If the People were willing to settle for a reasonable amount of time, do you think you could live with that?"

"Of course, it depends on what amount of 'time' the People would consider to be reasonable, and I would have to communicate it to my client, Your Honor. But I don't think the People have a slam dunk in this case."

"What's your time estimate, Ben?"

"Half day, Your Honor."

"Half day?"

"Yes."

"Why don't the two of you go out and talk about how to settle this thing."

"I don't think that any such discussions would be fruitful, Your Honor."

"For God's sake, Ben! You're lawyers, not gladiators, and there's no jury to play to here! Get out there and talk about the case. At the very least, see if you can stipulate any issues to narrow down the time in my courtroom today. And if you can't settle, you're number one on today's prelim calendar, so be ready to go."

Once outside the judge's chambers, the settlement discussion didn't take long. Taylor had no intention of giving a decent offer and Brent knew it. He stood there smugly and recited the phrase that Brent had told William he had expected to hear.

"If your client wants to plead guilty now and save the State some money, we can talk about life in prison instead of the death penalty," said Taylor in a casual manner, as if it was a foregone conclusion that William would be convicted and executed.

"Considering that they haven't executed anyone since 2006, and the constitutionality of California's death penalty is up in the air, that doesn't sound very much like a compromise to me," replied Brent.

81

Taylor wasn't going to push. It would be nice not to have to go through the ordeal of a trial to clinch this conviction; but, on the other hand, a trial would be good publicity to launch his campaign for D.A.

* * *

Taylor's first witness was Detective Salerno, who identified all of the police reports in his possession so they could be admitted into evidence. Since hearsay is allowed from police officers at preliminary hearings, Salerno's testimony probably would have been enough to hold William over for trial, but Taylor went the extra mile.

To Brent's delight, he called Officer John Albright himself. That would give Brent the opportunity to cross-examine him and evaluate his veracity as a witness. This was the first shooting incident for Officer Albright in an otherwise-clean record. But Brent suspected that there was more to his story than the pretty outer package revealed, and he had sent Jack to sniff out all the dirt he could find on Albright.

Albright took the witness stand in a crisp LAPD uniform which looked like it had just been taken off the dry cleaner's rack. William sat next to Brent at the counsel table, per Brent's request, but he still wore his prison skivvies and shackles.

"Officer Albright, on the 7th of October of this year, were you and Officer David Shermer on patrol on Burbank Boulevard in the San Fernando Valley?"

"Yes, sir, we were."

"And, did you have occasion on the night of October 7th to pull over the defendant, William Thomas?"

"Yes, sir."

"Have you filed a report with regard to this incident?"

"Yes, sir. I have."

"Showing you what has been marked for identification as People's Exhibit 1, can you identify this document as a true copy of your report?"

"Yes, sir. That is it."

"And does your report fully and accurately reflect what actually happened that night during the traffic stop that resulted in the death of Officer Shermer?"

"Yes, sir, it does."

"Your Honor, I move People's Exhibit 1 into evidence."

"Any objection?   Subject to cross examination, it will be received," boomed the baritone voice of Judge Hinman.

Taylor was sharp. The rules allowed him to present the police report in lieu of live testimony at the preliminary hearing. He was not going to allow Brent a preview of Albright's testimony at trial after all. But this decision had a double edge. It gave Brent the advantage of nailing down the details of Albright's version of the story to something he could not change at trial.

"Cross examination?"

"Thank you, Your Honor," said Brent. "Officer Albright, it says in your report that Mr. Thomas wrestled you to the ground; is that correct?"

"Yes, sir. It is."

William's lawyer's eyes were trained on Albright's. The cop averted his gaze from Brent's.

"And he wrestled you to the ground after you had hit him in the kneecap with your baton, isn't that correct?"

"Yes, sir, it is."

"You struck him in the knee hard enough to break it, didn't you?"

"Yes, sir."

"And it did disable him, didn't it?"

"Well, not entirely."

Just say yes!

"He lost the use of his knee, and he fell to the ground, isn't that true?"

"Well yes, but…"

The obvious question was, 'Yes, but what?', but Brent didn't want to give Albright the opportunity to expand on his answer.

"So your next move was to handcuff him, so he could pose no more threat to you or Officer Shermer's safety, isn't that correct?"

"Yes, sir. That is correct."

"Describe how you did that, please."

William leaned over to Brent, concerned. "I thought you weren't supposed to ask him anything you didn't know the answer to?"

"Usually, that's true," Brent said. "But I have a hunch that he doesn't know the answer to this question any more than we do. We need to pin him down to one story."

"Could you repeat the question, please?"

"Yes.   Describe how you attempted to handcuff Mr. Thomas."

"May I refer to my report?"

"I'd like your recollection please."

"I have no independent recollection other than what is stated in my report."

"Is that your answer?"

Taylor stood up.   "Your Honor, may we approach?"

Once at the bench, Taylor vehemently lodged his protest.

"Your Honor, there's no jury here."

Hinman squinted his furry salt and pepper eyebrow-covered eyes at Taylor.

"I know this is your show, Mr. Taylor, but Mr. Marks has the right to cross examine the witness."

Both the lawyers went back to their respective places.

"So, Officer Albright," Brent continued. "You don't remember where your body was in relation to Mr. Thomas's when you attempted to handcuff him and he wrestled you to the ground, is that correct?"

"That is correct."

"And you didn't hit Mr. Thomas in the ribs with your baton *before* he wrestled you to the ground, is that correct?"

"That is correct. He became violent. I had to subdue him. It occurred during the struggle."

"By wrestling you to the ground, do you mean that he was already on the ground and forced you down as well?"

"That is correct."

"So he didn't stand back up, correct?"

"No, sir."

"How did he pull you down?"

"He wrestled me to the ground," Albright repeated, looking a little confused.

"Move to strike as non-responsive, Your Honor."

"Sustained."

"With what did he wrestle you to the ground? His arms, his legs, his head?"

"Objection, compound!" interjected Taylor.

"Sustained."

"Did he bring you to the ground with his arms or his legs?"

"Both."

"Did he knock you off balance?"

"Yes, sir."

"How did he knock you off balance?"

Again, Brent asked an open-ended question. Taylor jumped up immediately.

"Objection, Your Honor. Counsel is using this hearing as a deposition."

"Overruled."

"He knocked me off balance with his arms and legs. He wrestled me to the ground."

"Did you have your handcuffs out before he knocked you off balance?"

"I can't recall."

"But you did attempt to handcuff him before he wrestled you to the ground, is that correct?"

"Yes I was about to."

"And after he wrestled you to the ground, you ended up on top of him, isn't that correct?"

"Yes."

"Describe how you did that?"

"I don't understand the question."

"It's a simple question, Mr. Albright. If the defendant wrestled you to the ground and you ended up on top of him, how did that happen? Did you land on top of him when he wrestled you to the ground?"

"Yes."

"And then you drew your weapon, isn't that correct?"

"I had my hand on my weapon, and withdrew it when I sensed that I was losing control of the suspect."

After extracting every painful detail of the struggle from Albright, Brent finally gave up and Taylor called the officers who appeared on the scene, who testified as to what they observed. Brent opted not to cross-examine them. Jack had already done a pretty good job in his interviews with them.

Taylor called a gun expert, who testified that the gun had been tampered with. Brent had no questions for this witness. He would need to retain his own gun expert to prepare a set of cross-examination questions. He hoped that

Taylor would not be tipped off to Brent's strategy by his questioning of Albright and the mechanics of the struggle.

The half day turned into a whole day, thanks in part to Brent's lengthy cross-examination of Albright. After all the evidence was in, Judge Hinman announced the result which didn't surprise anyone.

"The Court finds that sufficient evidence has been presented by the People to hold the Defendant to answer for the charge of capital murder."

Although Brent knew what the outcome would be, he couldn't shake the feeling that he was missing something. There seemed to be something that Taylor was holding back; but why, and, more importantly, what?

CHAPTER THIRTEEN

Two weeks after the preliminary hearing, the State of California filed an information charging William with capital murder and Brent entered a plea of not guilty. He tried again to get William released on bail, but it was again denied. At this point, since William did not waive his right to a speedy trial, the clock began ticking on a sixty day countdown to that trial.

Brent kept busy during this time – gathering evidence, interviewing witnesses - and Jack was looking for that nagging piece of the puzzle that Brent suspected was missing: the one he thought Taylor knew and was saving for something. If William could only regain his memory, it may solve the mystery. However, Dr. Reading wasn't making much progress with him.

Jack felt like a hamster running on a wheel. He was busy, but not getting anywhere, so he began to focus on the LAPD. As would be expected, Jack was not very popular with the crowd at the training academy bar.

The Los Angeles Police Revolver and Athletic Club Café was a bar and grill with a long history. Jack walked in, past the gift shop and the gun shop, and into the bar. When he took a calculated stool at the bar, it didn't take long for a chill to set into the room.

"I remember this place from my days in Metro before I joined the FBI," he said to a grey-haired man with a white shirt and yellow tie, sitting next to him.

"You're a fed?"

"Ex-FBI and ex-LAPD. Can I buy you a beer?"

"Only if you're drinking. Jerry Dalton," said the man, extending his hand.

"Jack Ruder," said Jack, completing the shake.

"Ruder. Aren't you the private dick working for that cop killer?"

"For Brent Marks, the lawyer for William Thomas."

"In that case, we don't have anything to say to each other," he said as the bartender put two tall ones in front of them.

Jack's choice of the 50s era diner for lunch and that particular seat was no accident. It was a little place right on the academy campus in Elysian Park, and its walls were littered with LAPD memorabilia. Although it was open to the public, most of the patrons were cops or trainees. Jerry Dalton was the Commander of the elite Metro Division, without his uniform, but Jack had recognized him from his file photo.

"Relax; have your beer. You don't have to talk to me."

"But I suppose you're going to try."

"Of course," Jack said, lifting up his mug. "Cheers."

"Cheers."

"There's just something bothering me about this case."

Dalton just looked ahead as he sipped his beer, indicating he was listening but may not care to comment or answer.

"What was a Metro unit assigned to North Hollywood doing on Burbank Blvd. in Sherman Oaks?"

"Our officer's been cleared by Force Investigation Division. Why should I care what they were doing on Burbank Blvd.?"

"I know, I know; but if you look at the force involved, does it really set well with you? Metro can't afford an incident like the Rampart scandal. If this is one bad apple, I would think you'd want to know."

"I suppose your fancy Santa Barbara lawyer is going to spin it that way," said Dalton, downing the rest of his beer in one gulp as he pushed off. "Thanks for the beer."

Jack asked around to see what he could turn up, if anything. It was enough to make everyone there uncomfortable to the point he was starting to feel like a nuisance himself. He finally figured that this was a dead end, and set off to serve subpoenas on Albright's fellow members in the Metro Division. At this point he was out of ideas, so he just decided to shake as many trees as he could to see what would fall out.

CHAPTER FOURTEEN

Dr. Reading was frustrated. The attorney visiting room in the Men's Central Jail was no place to conduct a decent clinical examination. She showed the videos to William on her iPad to try to jar his memory.

"I'm sorry, Doc, but you're just wasting your time."

"I don't think so, William. In most cases of post-traumatic stress disorder, the memory loss is temporary. I want you to look at the videos and tell me as much as you remember."

William watched the video clips over and over, but nothing seemed to spur his memory.

"Nothing, Doc."

"That's okay. Let's repeat."

* * *

After Jack finished making himself public enemy number one with the LAPD's Metro Division, he joined Brent back in Santa Barbara at the video editor's lab to watch the enhanced videos. The video technician, a graduate of Brooks Institute, had brightened the contrast and reconstructed information from the data that was available on the original tapes, then spliced them together in chronological order. In a small viewing theater, Jack and Brent sat in the first row while the new video was projected onto a screen.

"The quality of the technology is good," said the technician. "It's just the lack of ambient light that makes it grainy and pixilated in places. I reconstructed what I could from the digital information we had so we can see the detail better."

The video was 100% better than it was before, but it was still not perfect, and, since it was taken in 10 second intervals, a lot of what had really happened was not even recorded. Hopefully, if Dr. Reading's therapy with William worked, he could fill in the blanks.

"Stop there!" said Brent, at a point in the video where Albright was on top of William. "Can you play it from here frame by frame?"

"Sure."

"There! See that, Jack?"

"Yeah, I do. He's pulling out his gun."

"But look where the handcuffs are."

"I don't see them."

"Stop. Go back a couple of frames," Brent said to the technician. "Stop. Can you blow this part up here?"

"Sure."

"See the handcuffs now, Jack?

"Yeah. They're still on his belt, in the case."

"Right. He's sitting on William and, instead of reaching for his handcuffs, he pulls his gun."

* * *

William spent as much time in the jail law library as he could, doing legal research. He sent letters to Brent every day, summarizing the cases he had found. Several of the inmates who frequented the library themselves had asked

William to help them with their cases, but he always politely declined, until he ran into Curly and his entourage. Curly was not accustomed to taking no for an answer.

"Whattaya mean you ain't no criminal lawyer? You a lawyer, right? And you in here, that means you also a criminal."

Curly was a tall, bald black man with big hands. He wore the sleeves of his scrubs rolled up, exposing his enormous biceps, which were covered with gang tattoos.

"The thing is, Curly, I'm still licensed. If I do legal research for you, or give an opinion, that makes me your lawyer."

"So what? That's what I want."

"It creates potential professional responsibility issues for me."

"What I seen, you already got issues." Curly laughed, and his three buddies laughed with him in chorus.

"I'm sorry, Curly."

"Man, you don't know sorry," said Curly, who shoved over a stack of books William had placed on his table as he turned and left. His buddies stared William down, flashing gang signs as they slowly backed away.

I hope he calms down.

* * *

William waited in line at the cafeteria as the trustees dished out food for dinner. As soon as his tray was full of slop, he made a beeline to his table. A group of men in dreadlocks taunted him as he walked by.

"You think you're tough, cop killer: eat this!" said one of them, grabbing at his crotch.

"Settle down over there!" called out a Sheriff's Deputy who was supervising the cafeteria.

As William prepared to sit down, two men jumped up in front of him and two in back of him. One of the men in front slapped his tray upward and the food went flying, raining down mashed potatoes and meatballs all over the next table and causing an instant riot.

As the guards ran to address the disturbance, a free-for-all broke out among the inmates. Like a bar fight from an old Western, a group of about 80 slugged it out with each other as the guards sounded the alarm and the other inmates, not wanting to be involved, shuffled off to the deputies' calls for lockdown.

William was stuck in the middle of the melee with no way out. Suddenly he was grabbed from behind under his arms in a wrestling hold as another inmate appeared in front of him, bearing a home-made knife, which he thrust at William's stomach. William winced and tried to move out of the way.

* * *

As Brent prepared William's defense, he pored through cases of excessive force not just from California, but from every jurisdiction in the States, to find anything similar fact-wise that may apply to William's case. He followed all the library leads that William had sent, even though he had already uncovered most of them himself.

In the jail, William used the traditional research method that Brent had learned in law school, which involved sorting through large bound indexes, then cases; each kept in their own hardbound volume, while Brent was speeding through key words in the legal research program on his computer. He had forgotten about his lunch date with Angela, since he was so involved in the research and taking care of some other cases that had been languishing since he had been concentrating so much on William's, and the day had flown by before he had even realized it.

At six o'clock, Brent's eyes began burning and his stomach churned. Melinda had locked up an hour earlier and Brent hadn't even heard her leave. He glanced at the clock in the right bottom side of his screen and realized that it was time to go home. By the time he reached his neighborhood in Harbor Hills, the sun was making a spectacular light show as it bedded itself down over the ocean.

Brent saw that Angela's car was in the driveway. *Did we have a date tonight? Did I forget?* As he stepped inside, Calico whisked by, disinterested. She stopped and casually looked at Brent, stretched and yawned, and continued on her way without giving him the usual "welcome home" greeting. Angela had obviously already fed her.

The wonderful mixture of veal osso bucco, tomatoes, carrots and onions led Brent to the kitchen, where he found Angela busy brewing up a special gourmet meal.

"I hope I didn't mess up any date plans."

Angela turned away from the stove, and hugged Brent with her arms, as her hands were occupied with a spoon and a dish towel. She kissed him.

"You actually did, and I was really angry with you. I almost didn't show up here, but I decided to have our date anyway."

"Sorry," Brent said, making his best puppy dog face.

Angela put her hands on her hips. "I decided to forgive you, but don't you dare do it again."

"I'm so sorry."

Angela put down her instruments, washed her hands, and led Brent outside to the patio, where two glasses of red wine presided over a spread of Italian appetizers. Brent sat down under the toasty canopy of the outdoor heater.

"When you didn't show up and you didn't call, I was angry at first, but decided to show you what you've been missing."

"This is a great way to get even," said Brent. "And better than any restaurant. I promise I won't miss the next one."

CHAPTER FIFTEEN

There was no time for William to react, although he saw his fate unfolding as if in slow motion. The knife was moving so fast he only saw a gleam of light reflected off it. Then, as suddenly as it was thrust at him, a pair of strong hands pulled him back as his attacker was disarmed by another.

"Now you owe me, bro," said Curly as he dragged William to safety while a group of guards pounced on the disarmed aggressor.

* * *

Jack started early the next morning, following the cold leads he had developed on Officer

Albright.   None of the cops in the Metro Division were willing to discuss Albright with him, so Jack went back to Captain Tennyson, who lent him an ear.

"I've got five minutes, Jack. What's up?"

"Marty, I've been trying to do a background on Albright, but nobody's talking. I need to know who his buddies are, who his partners are, everything about him, to do my job on this case."

"No surprise to me that nobody's talking."

"Me neither, but it seems to me that this goes beyond a code of silence.   They're hiding something."

"Then you should go see the Commanding Officer of IAG."

IAG was the LAPD's internal affairs department, in charge of investigating all kinds of police corruption.

* * *

Brent focused on the enhanced videos, which he kept watching over and over, frame by frame, to try to catch every detail.

"You think something is there and you're just not seeing it?" asked Angela.

"Exactly. It has to be here; or at least a part of it. Why would Albright pull his gun after he had subdued William? Why wouldn't he just handcuff him?"

"Having been in the field myself, you really can't use hindsight to examine an officer's actions. We have to act quickly, and sometimes on little or no information."

Angela was an FBI agent, currently assigned to the Santa Barbara office.

"I know, Angie, but look at the way Albright's moving. Doesn't it seem like he's acting more out of emotion than reacting to a dangerous situation?"

"It's hard to tell. Play it back for me from the beginning."

Angela paid careful attention to every detail of the video, then asked for a playback, then a playback with stops.

"I can see this video matching both your witnesses' story and Officer Albright's," she said. "There's just not enough detail to see what happened unless you were there."

Brent had to agree. The video would be no turning point in the trial.

The Commanding Officer of the Internal Affairs Group was more receptive to Jack than even Marty Tennyson. Commander Jeffrey Owen was a long time veteran of the LAPD with the most hated job in the department. He had made his way up the ranks of the department the hard way: with effort, integrity and plain old hard work, as opposed to politics. That was part of the reason behind his unwavering incorruptibility.

Jack waited for Owen in the waiting room to his office, which was spartan in its décor, displaying framed photographs of Owen posing with police chiefs all the way back to Ed Davis. As Jack was shown into his office, Owen glanced up from his reports and greeted him.

"Marty Tennyson said you had something of interest for IAG."

"It's just a hunch of mine, Commander Owen."

Jack knew that Owen was the type who operated on his instincts. In his world, where the police were policing their own, often small, inexplicable insights were the only way to reveal evidence. To Jack's surprise, Owen looked like a graying Joe Friday from "Dragnet," with fleshy jowls, furry eyebrows, and a forehead that had never seen a drop of Botox. And he spoke in that Joe Friday nasal tone.

"I always take hunches seriously in my business, especially when they come from a respected bureau man. So this is about the Albright case?"

"Yes. I've been trying to interview all the officers who worked with Officer Albright, but, not only do they seem to be a tight-lipped group, I have a feeling they're all holding back something."

"As insightful as your intuition may be, we can't really use it as the basis for a complaint or an investigation. Do you have any concrete facts to back up your feelings?"

"I have two sworn statements from witnesses on the scene who say that Albright used unreasonable force in dealing with my client."

"Your client, the one who is accused of murdering Officer Shermer?"

"Yes; but the bottom line is that if Officer Albright was acting illegally, my client had the right to defend himself, and that means that Officer Albright would be ultimately responsible for his partner's death."

"So you're asking me to help you prove your client's case?"

"No, sir. That is the context of my investigation, but all I'm asking you is to help me find out the truth."

Jack could see from Owen's furrowed brows that he was processing all the information.

"That's all you have? And your eyewitnesses, I understand, were under the influence of alcohol at the time, is that right?"

"Yes, but too many things don't add up."

"Like what?"

"We've enhanced the video footage. It appears that Officer Albright drew his weapon on my client, even after he had control over him, without attempting to handcuff him."

"Hence, your excessive force claim."

"Yes, and there's the question of what they were doing there in the first place. Why is a specialized Metro unit assigned to North Hollywood alone in Sherman Oaks for no apparent reason?"

"All interesting questions – but not enough for me to launch any kind of inquiry. Tell you what, Ruder, keep me posted. And I'll ask around and see if I can open some doors for you."

"Thank you, sir."

CHAPTER SIXTEEN

Melinda called from the office on Brent's home line.

"Boss, are you coming in soon? Mr. Thomas has been calling from the jail. There was some trouble."

"Keep taking his calls and tell him I'll be there in fifteen minutes."

Brent rushed into the office just in time to receive William's call from the jail. The entire population was on lockdown. William had only minor injuries, but life for a reputed cop killer was not very good in the central jail. The guards had no desire to protect him, and the inmates all saw his reputation as a potential challenge.

"I found some more cases for you Brent, and it looks like now I've been enlisted as a jailhouse lawyer, so I'm not sure how much time I'll have to work on my own case."

"Send me the citations by mail and I'll look them up. How's it coming with Dr. Reading?"

"Nothing's happening there."

"I'm going to give her the enhanced video to show you. Maybe it will help you fill in the blanks."

"Brent, if I can't remember what happened…"

"Then we can't put you on the stand, period. You have to remember, William. It may make the difference between freedom and a lifetime in prison."

"And they always taught me in law school that you were innocent until proven guilty."

"That's how it's worded, but whoever wrote the rules must have had dyslexia, because it's certainly the opposite in application."

* * *

The wind stung William's face as he ran. He felt the sweat on his neck and the fear in his heart.

"Run, William, run!"

He heard TJ yelling in front of him, and heard the dogs barking behind him. He could see the river straight ahead. Get to the river – the dogs won't catch your scent. *William looked behind and caught a glimpse of a shotgun.*

"There's the nigger!" he heard someone say in the distance. William ran, hit something hard with his foot, stumbled, struck his knee on a big rock, and fell face first into the dirt. He scrambled to get up, but couldn't. Must be broken. Got to crawl to the river. *As William dragged his body through the dusty path toward the river, the sound of the dogs howling and the men approaching became louder and louder. He struggled as he crawled through the dirt to the sandy riverbank. Then he felt a shooting pain in his knee, like it was on fire, and a firm grip on his ankle, pulling the leg with the broken knee.*

William's aggressor turned him over. He was a uniformed policeman, with his pistol pointed straight at William's face. William grabbed the pistol, wrenched it out of the cop's hands, turned it on the cop and fired.

"It was me! I did it!" William screamed, and sat up in his bunk, his neck drenched with sweat.

"Shut up fool! You'll wake up the whole cell block!" said his cell mate, as he struck William's bunk with his foot.

I did it. I shot the cop.

CHAPTER SEVENTEEN

"I'm guilty, Brent. You can't put me on the stand."

Brent looked in disbelief at his client. Usually they professed their innocence and he had his doubts. In this case, it was the opposite.

"William, talk to Dr. Reading. You can't base your perception of this entire case on a dream you had."

"But it was so real, Brent. I really thought I was innocent, I really did. I'm going to miss everything – teaching Danny to ride a bike, playing ball, Sissy's wedding."

"Now, knock it off. You're forgetting about intent. You didn't intend to kill Officer Shermer, did you?"

"No, but I swear to God, I intended to kill the other one. What is it you said about transferred intent?"

"Not if you were defending yourself and Albright's actions were illegal."

"That's just it, Brent. I'm not entirely sure if I was defending myself. Maybe I just couldn't take any more and I just let loose the animal inside me."

"We all have that animal inside of us, William."

* * *

Acting on a tip from Commander Owen, Jack went to a local Los Angeles bar which members of the Metro Division were known to frequent on Wednesdays, their paydays. They used to hang out and blow off steam at the Academy Bar, but ever since a motorcycle cop was killed in a drunk driving incident on a Wednesday night, the bar was closed on paydays and they had to take the party elsewhere.

The Stars and Bars was similar to other police bars that had been popular with cops and firemen throughout the years. Its walls were lined with badges, uniforms, and black and white historical photographs, and every shelf and table was packed with police memorabilia.

Seated at the bar were four officers wearing "tuxedos," which consisted of their uniform pants and white T-shirts. It was the traditional garb for Metro officers on payday. Jack took a seat at the bar and ordered a Corona with lime. When the bartender slid it over to him, Jack popped the lime into the bottle and raised it in a toast to his neighbors.

"You don't like American beer?" asked a blond-haired cop next to him. The rest of them chuckled.

"Not really, actually. I guess that separates us bureau men from you guys."

"You a G-Man?"

"Retired. I'm also ex-LAPD. Jack Ruder." Jack offered his hand, which the blond cop shook with a smile.

"I'm a private detective now. Working on the Albright case."

The blond cop's smile faded into disgust. "This conversation's over," he said, and stared ahead as if Jack didn't exist. The cop next to him glared at Jack.

Jack slid his card to them on the bar. "In case you change your mind and want to talk."

"We won't."

"It could get pretty hot for you guys. Better to come clean now."

"Is that a threat?"

"Just a fact," Jack said, as he set his bottle down on the bar and walked away.

* * *

Brent had an appointment with Gregory Samuelson, a ballistics expert. Samuelson was a nerdy little forensics analyst who had previously served as a police officer for the Los Angeles Sheriff's department, and worked in the forensics lab before he retired into private industry. He asked for all the police reports, witness statements, and video and audio tapes for his preliminary evaluation. Brent turned over duplicates of the information and Samuelson looked through them to determine what was there. He looked at Brent through his coke-bottle glasses.

"I can analyze all this data and give you an honest report of what I think happened, all at my regular hourly rate, and then you can decide whether to hire me or not; fair enough?"

"Sounds good to me."

After the appointment with Samuelson, Brent went back to the office where Jack was waiting for him.

"Hey Jack, any luck with the testosterone club?"

"Very funny. Did you forget you're talking to an ex-cop?"

"That's impossible to forget, Jack. No matter how you try, you can never disguise the fact that you will always look like a cop. I'll bet your parents knew that you would be a cop when you were two years old."

Jack followed Brent into his office and took a seat in the wooden chair in front of Brent's desk.

"It can't be that they're just covering for Albright. There's something more," he said.

"Anything concrete?"

"No, still just a hunch, but something stinks over there."

CHAPTER EIGHTEEN

Sarah Thomas sat in the waiting room at Brent's office, nervously scrolling through images on her phone to pass the time. Finally, Brent opened the door and walked out with Jack.

"Sarah, hello," said Brent. "I wasn't expecting to see you today."

"Hello, Brent," said Sarah as she stood up.

"This is Jack Ruder. He's the investigator working on William's case."

Sarah and Jack exchanged pleasantries, and Jack went back to his investigation.

"Please, come in," said Brent.

Sarah took a seat in the office as Brent eased back behind his desk. She looked fragile and worn out, not like the Sarah he had known from the Bar Association meetings with William; but her beauty shone through all the despair.

"So, how can I help you today?"

Sarah reached into her purse and pulled out her checkbook.

"I just came by to give you a check."

"Sarah, you could have mailed that. What's really up?"

Sarah's lip quivered, and she tightened up to cut off the oncoming flurry of tears.

"I'm worried, Brent. William's convinced that he's guilty of killing that cop. You're not going to plead him guilty, are you?"

"Of course not. He's working with one of the best psychiatric specialists in the country. I can't discuss my conversations with William or it will break our attorney-client privilege, but I can tell you that we have not changed our defense."

"What do you think the chances are?"

"That's something I really can't predict with certainty, but, with or without William's testimony, I think we have a solid defense and our chances are good."

Tears dropped from the corner of Sarah's eyes as she reached for a Kleenex from her purse.

"The kids keep asking when Daddy's coming home and I don't know what to tell them. I can't believe this is happening to us."

"You can help William, Sarah. Stay strong, think positively and we'll be on the other side of this before you know it."

"I'll try."

"Start planning William's homecoming."

Sarah managed to break through her sadness with a tiny smile of hope.

* * *

Commander Owen had been kind enough to give Jack a list of the tight-lipped members of Officer Albright's Metro squad. Jack had put that list to good use all day, but it wasn't until the night shift that his espionage started to pay off.

As Jack sat in his plain-looking Ford Taurus eating an In-N-Out burger and listening to police dispatcher calls, he heard, "15-Robert-7, requesting Code 7 at Burbank and Coldwater."

"Stand by," crackled the dispatcher, followed by "15-Robert-7, okay for 7."

Jack rolled to the location just in time to witness the patrol unit taking off toward Van Nuys on Burbank Blvd. He fell in behind them, following at a long enough distance not to be noticed. *Police units are supposed to stay in their reported location for lunch breaks. Why did they check out for a lunch break and go to a different location outside their area?* 15-Robert-7 was now off the grid.

CHAPTER NINETEEN

"Is there something I can do to help you with this case?" asked Angela, more out of curiosity than anything else, as she sipped on her tea.

"You mean the FBI or you personally?"

"Both. Of course, the bureau can't get involved unless it's something we're working on."

"That may come to be, actually. Jack seems to think there is something fishy going on with Albright's Metro squadron, but he can't quite put his finger on it."

"Police corruption? Like the Rampart scandal in the 90s?"

"Maybe. If we can find something to hang an investigation on, maybe one of them would talk. They all had to know that Albright was a hothead."

"What about his family and friends?"

"Same story. Jack tried, and nobody's talking."

"I'm sure Jack has looked into his background."

"He's a Boy Scout."

"You must not be seeing something, Brent. Give me Jack's reports and let me follow up. Maybe I can find the missing link."

* * *

Jack followed 15-Robert-7 as the cruiser pulled up alongside some fleabag motels on Sepulveda Blvd. and waited. He found a vantage point, pulled out his night vision binoculars, and focused on the car. Nothing unusual. The two cops were just sitting in the front seat, apparently waiting for something or somebody. They weren't eating lunch.

After about five minutes, a girl came out of one of the motel cabins and began to turn on Sepulveda. The girl came over to their passenger side window. She was 20-something, with heavy makeup and a cheesy, partially see-through red mini-dress – obviously a working girl. *It wouldn't be the first time for a cop to look the other way for prostitution. For favors?* The girl got into the back of the cruiser and it took off. Jack followed suit.

When the police car finally halted on a desolate side street, Jack focused his binoculars on the girl in the back, who handed the officers something – looked like an envelope - and then left. The black and white was off again; this time to another location on Sepulveda, where it repeated the same scene with another hooker. This time, Jack hung back after they left and decided to question the girl. He switched on his digital recorder, pulled up alongside her, moving slowly, and rolled down his window.

"Hi," he said to the girl. She was red haired, light-eyed and quite young.

"Hi. Want a date?" she asked, batting her doll-like black eyelashes.

"Sure."

The girl came up to Jack's car and leaned in the passenger side window.

"What were you looking for?"

"I don't know. Depends on the price."

"You know how many yards in a football field?" The girl smiled seductively.

"Yeah."

"Well, it'll run you about three football fields."

"What about something less than – um, everything?"

"Are you a cop or something?"

"No."

"Well, you seem like a nice guy. Why don't we drive around the corner and park? If you want, like a blow job or something, it's only one football field."

"Deal, hop in."

Jack opened the door and the girl got into the passenger side. She smelled like a mixture of soap and strong perfume.

"What's your name, honey?"

Jack flashed took out his wallet and flashed his private-eye license.

"Jack Ruder, and you're in big trouble, young lady," Jack said, in his best cop face. "I'm investigating police corruption, and I've been watching you with those two cops back there."

The girl's face registered a mixture of panic and fear.

"Please, please, they'll kill me if they knew I was talking to you. Just let me go," she begged, like a little girl. "We can make a deal. They get it for free; so can you."

Jack felt bad for the young prostitute, but kept up the pressure.

"We know what's going on with those Metro cops, and you're in it thick enough to do serious prison time for conspiracy."

"No, I don't have anything to do with it, I swear. I just collect the money from the girls and give it to them! You have to believe me! Tears pooled in her eyes and cascaded in rivers of melted black mascara down her powdered cheeks.

"You said they'd kill you if they found out. Did they tell you that?"

"There's one who's really crazy. He put my girlfriend in the hospital."

"Is this him?" Jack asked, holding up a picture of Albright.

"Yeah, that's the guy. There's something wrong with him."

"Who did he beat up?"

"My girlfriend, Tiffany. That's her street name. I don't know her real one."

"What did she do to get him so riled up?"

"That's just it – nothing! He just roughed her up because he could – because she said or did something that pissed him off. He used to call her his favorite nigger. Everyone thought he was a psycho. And one day after he spent a couple hours in her room, he busted her up really bad you know? Told her if she ratted on him, he would kill her."

"Where can I find her?"

"I don't know. Can you let me go now?"

CHAPTER TWENTY

William looked with frustration at Dr. Reading. She could see in his eyes that he felt that all this therapy was a waste of time.

"William, I can help you; but you have to meet me halfway. You have to try."

William looked down.

"One thing I learned in here, Doc, is that there're no happy endings to anything. I'm going to tell Brent to plead me out and just take my chances."

"William, I don't think your dream is a repressed memory."

"Oh yeah? Then tell me something – why do I keep having that same dream, over and over again?"

"It's nothing more than an expression of your anger toward Officer Albright. You shot *him* in your dream, right? Not his partner?"

"Yeah, and I keep shooting him. Every time."

Dr. Reading put on her reading glasses and shifted through the files in her briefcase.

"I did some research on this type of dream. It could indicate not only anger toward Albright, but that you feel you've been victimized. I'd like to put you under hypnosis, William; perhaps with the aid of some hypnotic drugs."

"You can't do that here."

"No, but I'm going to ask Brent if he can get a court order to allow this type of therapy, and then we can transfer you to the hospital to do it."

"Then, wouldn't they know what was going on with my head? I thought we were going to keep my sessions with you private."

"That's right. We don't want to reveal your therapy at this point, unless you don't remember anything and they have to call me as a witness.

It would be best if your memory recovers and you can tell your story yourself."

"Then how do we get this court order without blowing our cover, so to speak?"

"Maybe Brent can do it in confidence, since it involves doctor-patient confidentiality, and, even more, because of attorney-client privilege. You can't really tell your attorney everything he needs to know unless you've recovered from your PTSD."

"Okay, go ahead: see what you can do."

* * *

Jack met with Brent and told him of the breakthrough he had in the case. He recounted the interview with Trixy, the young prostitute, and turned over all of her identification information.

"Great job, Jack. We need to get her served with a subpoena for trial before she skips out on us."

"I'll serve her tonight."

"Great. What else will you do with this lead?"

"I'll take it to Owen over at IAG and see what he wants to do about it, if anything."

"What did she do when she found out you weren't a cop?"

"Turned from a crying little girl into a harpy. Screamed at me that I would be sorry."

"In that case, Jack, watch your back."

"I will."

* * *

Thanks to the recognition of the psychotherapist-patient privilege in California law, Brent was able to make a motion to allow the transfer of William to County Hospital to undergo psychotherapy without revealing the nature of the therapy. The motion was granted, and William was transferred for an indefinite period, until Dr. Reading released him or until his trial date, whichever came first. This came as a great relief to William, until word got out that he would be leaving the jail. All night the night before, the inmates in his block taunted him with a cacophony of unpleasant sounds. Unable to sleep, he just lay in bed listening to them, afraid if he closed his eyes, someone would sneak up on him and slit his throat. All night long he could hear them taunting him, threatening to kill him and make it look like suicide.

"Cop killer's goin' to the Ding Wing!"

"You gonna dance on the blacktop, they'll think you done the Dutch!"

The threats wound down as the night marched on toward dawn, and William fought to keep his eyes open, which was becoming more and more difficult. As he slipped into unconsciousness, he realized he was suffocating.

Officer Albright sat on William's chest and pointed his gun in his face. William panicked. He gasped for air, felt the blood draining from his brain. With his final effort, he turned the gun on Albright and fired, hitting him in the chest.

William's eyes opened wildly, breathing heavily, his heart pounding. The dreams were changing.

CHAPTER TWENTY ONE

Brent spent the precious time leading up to the trial putting together his trial notebooks, which would contain every voir dire outline for jury selection, every direct and cross-examination outline for every witness, and all the evidence. He researched the law on excessive force and crafted jury instructions that he would ask the Judge to read to the jury before their deliberation.

From time to time Jack would check in and give Brent a copy of his reports on the latest lead he was working on, so Brent could stay up to date in his preparation. But there were still gaping holes in the big picture, which was what really happened that night. Jack was working on filling those holes on the outside, and Dr. Reading was working on them from the inside with William.

Under hypnosis, William was able to recall every detail of the night Officer Shermer was shot, up until the point that Albright used bodily force.

"He's on top of me. What does he want from me?"

"Calm down William, we're just recalling memories. What's happening now?"

"I don't know! I don't know!"

"Try, William, try!"

William moved his head from side to side, violently. He grimaced and coughed.

"I can't breathe!"

All of a sudden William woke up, sweating profusely. He reached for a glass of water and downed it.

"Do you have any recall?"

"Only bits and pieces. It was like I was living it all over again."

Unfortunately, even with the use of hypnotic drug therapy, nothing was unlocking the door to the memories which William's subconscious had shoved into the deepest reaches of his brain.

The nightmares, however, did continue. It seemed to Dr. Reading that William's brain was trying to tell him something, because the dreams were always about violence and always involved a gun in William's hands.

"Memories are not like recordings on a computer. That's why, when you have flashbacks about that night, it seems like it's real to you; like a real memory. We have to help your brain reprocess the memory, so it sees it as something in the past and not something happening right now. Do you understand?"

"Yes."

"Good. I'd like to try something else. It may seem kind of simple or silly to you, but I think it may help. It's called eye movement desensitization and reprocessing."

"Okay; anything you think may help."

"Just lie back and let your body go limp. I want you to think about that night, and only that night."

William lay back and tried to relax. He put his arms to his sides.

"Now, I'm going to pass my hand back and forth across your face. Follow the movements with your eyes, but don't stop thinking about what happened that night. It should help your brain to reprocess the event."

The session continued for about half an hour.

"It's no use, doctor. I'm not remembering anything."

"Don't worry. This is going to take some time."

"I think we've ran out of that, Doc."

CHAPTER TWENTY TWO

It was the day before trial, and it seemed to Brent that nothing was in place. His client had undergone intensive therapy with Dr. Reading at the hospital, but still had no memory of the incident and still believed himself to be guilty. Now William was ushered back to the main jail, where he was put into the general population, contrary to Brent's requests. Jack had located a witness who might help run down leads on Albright, but she was a hooker who could easily leave town on the next Greyhound. Still, Brent had to be ready for any contingency, and he stayed late at the office preparing his voir dire and cross-examination.

The theory of the case was simple. If Brent could discredit Albright, and he was the only one who would testify that William shot his partner, then it would be impossible for the D.A. to prove beyond a reasonable doubt that William was the shooter. That all depended on Jack. The alternative argument, which was the most difficult one, was that William shot back in self-defense, intending only to shoot Albright, and the bullet sought an unintended victim. That was only a good defense if the jury believed that the force Albright used was excessive.

The jury would be composed of 12 people from the area surrounding the Van Nuys branch of the Los Angeles Superior Court. This bothered Brent the most. The demographic of that area consisted of industrial workers, hospital workers, and employees of large companies, such as the telephone company; and Brent didn't expect the jury to be very colorful. Taylor would exercise every peremptory challenge he had to kick any person of color off the jury. After the O.J. Simpson case, it was standard modus operandi for prosecutors.

Brent had the trial organized into notebooks, which contained all of his outlines and every piece of evidence at the flip of a tab. However, even though he had prepared thoroughly, he knew to always expect surprises.

* * *

Jack waited for Trixy's john to leave, then knocked on the door of cabin 7 at the Starlight Motel on Sepulveda Blvd. Trixy opened the door, realized who it was, then attempted to close it against Jack's protruding foot.

"Charlotte Rutherford, this is for you," Jack said, as he handed her the subpoena."

The girl threw the subpoena back at him and said, "You've made enough trouble for me. What if I just don't remember anything?"

"That's the funny thing about memory. Technology has a way of making us never forget things."

Jack switched on his digital recorder, and played back her words. *Everyone thought he was a psycho. And one day he busted her up really bad you know? Told her if she ratted on him, he would kill her.*

Jack turned and left. Their primary witness at this point was a young prostitute whom nobody knew by her real name. She could disappear in a few hours easier than William's memory had left him.

When Jack went back to his car, he noticed that his right rear tire had gone flat.

"Shit," he said to himself, as he pondered whether to call Triple-A and wait for an hour for them to come or to get a can of fixit and blow it up himself until he could get to a gas station. He opted for the second choice and began to walk to a nearby 7-Eleven store, which was just a couple of blocks away.

As Jack passed a dimly lit cross street, he heard something down the street that sounded like someone was hurt, or in trouble. He turned away from his path to investigate. In the bushes, about 100 yards away, he heard a woman's voice, calling "Help me! Help me!"

Jack followed the sound of the voice to the entrance of a small alley and there, among the trash cans, was a girl, sprawled out among the garbage cans. It looked as if she had been beaten. Jack bent over to check on the girl.

"Thank God you came. They beat me up. Be careful, they might still be…"

Jack never had the chance to pick up the girl to take her to safety because, all of a sudden, he was kicked off balance. He stood up to defend himself and came face to face with four men wearing dark clothing and ski masks. Jack withdrew his gun, but one of the men kicked it out of his hand and the gun discharged. They surrounded him, each punching and kicking as

Jack attempted to ward off every blow. They slammed him against a trash can and he fell to the ground.

"So you want to play with guns, huh?" asked one of the men, taking out his own handgun and pointing it at Jack's face.

The man was panting hard like a big dog, and his hands were shaking.

"Put it away!" said another. We have to go!"

The man with the gun wouldn't budge. One of his buddies put his hand on his shoulder and said, "Don't do it. It'll fuck everything up."

Jack heard a ringing in his ears, but through the ringing, he also heard the sound of an approaching helicopter in the distance.

"Hurry! Now!" said one of the men. The one with the gun pocketed it and said, "This isn't over.", and he kicked Jack repeatedly until the lights went out in his head.

CHAPTER TWENTY THREE

The Van Nuys Courthouse West was a modern building that had been erected in the 90s to replace the old facility, which was a small, rundown 60s-era building whose population had outgrown it. As a consequence, it had expanded into a series of bungalows all around the property, which had acted as temporary courtrooms for years. In those days Brent's mentor, Charles Stinson, had a "mobile office" parked outside the old courthouse where he saw clients in between hearings. Before the rules for attorney advertising had been revised (allowing lawyers to advertise on television), Charles had gotten into trouble with a local judge who felt that having "Law Office of Charles Stinson" printed on the back of the van was in violation of the solicitation rules. The judge filed a complaint with the California Bar, which Charles resolved by painting over his name and offering to send the Judge a picture of his "bare rear end." Charles was never afraid to go up against any type of adversary, no matter what. It had been several years since he died of cancer at the young age of 83, but Brent remembered him every time he went into a big trial. Charles was bigger than life and a great inspiration for any trial lawyer; but especially for Brent, who had started practicing law under his wing.

The new building had come just in time to serve the public's needs, only to be followed by an economic crisis that had forced the County to cut court staff and reduce working hours. Department N was identical to all the other courtrooms. It was small, modern, and had a clean, almost antiseptic look which contrasted with the corridors which were a cross-section of human misery, whether it be from poverty, drugs, alcohol, or a combination of any or all of them. Judge Adam Schwartz ran a tight ship and did not tolerate tardiness, so Brent arrived well before the doors opened.

Jack wasn't there, and Brent had been unable to reach him on his cell phone. It was absolutely critical to William's case to know whether Jack had been able to finally serve Trixy and whether he could stake out her location to make sure she didn't skip out on the subpoena, which ordered her to appear on the first day of trial. If Jack could bring her in, Judge Schwartz could order her back on the day of Brent's case-in-chief.

Sarah arrived with two of William's best lawyer-like suits, to dress him for the trial. Appearances were everything for a jury. It was important for them not to see "just another prisoner" in a jumpsuit, but a successful, functioning member of society. Sarah sat down next to Brent on a bench outside the courtroom. She was dressed conservatively, but nicely, as if she was going to a job interview or a PTA meeting. The jury would discover who she was, and her presence as well as her appearance was just as important as William's, even though she was the wrong color (for them.)

"Brent, I brought the clothes, but I'm so nervous I feel as if I'm going to throw up."

"That's normal, Sarah. Trials aren't fun. I often feel the same right before one."

"You do?"

"Yes, but don't worry." He touched her hand. We're well prepared, and I'm not going to throw up."

That brought a little smile out of Sarah. Brent opened his briefcase and pulled out one of his trial notebooks to show her. He opened it to the tab marked "voir dire."

"This is where we'll start today, with jury selection, after the judge has had a chance to go over all his rules with us."

When the Bailiff finally opened the doors to Department N at about ten to nine, Jack was still nowhere to be found. Brent hung behind the people shuffling into the courtroom to make one last phone call to try to reach him, but it went straight to voice mail.

Benjamin Taylor came into the courtroom, looking confident and ready for battle, shortly before the Judge took the bench, after having bathed in the river of reporters outside the courthouse which Brent had avoided completely by coming in early. Judge Schwartz would have no cameras in his courtroom: only reporters and sketch artists. He was not going to have an O.J. Simpson trial on his hands.

Before he took the bench, Schwartz called the attorneys into chambers for a pretrial conference. Seated at his desk without his robes, he greeted Brent and Taylor in a friendly manner. It was the first time Brent would appear before Judge Schwartz, who was a short, balding man who appeared to be in his 60s. Jack's background check showed him to be a former prosecutor, like most of the other judges in the Superior Court who had succeeded in being reelected on a "tough on crime" platform.

"Hello, gentlemen; please come in."

Brent and Taylor had a seat in the two chairs in front of the judge's desk. The judge eyed both of them. Despite his reputation, Brent had the impression that he was a fair jurist. He didn't put on airs and he smiled as if he was at a local Bar Association meeting among friends.

"We've already done all the preliminaries: are you two ready to pick a jury?"

"Yes," replied Taylor.

"As soon as I can get my client into some decent clothes," responded Brent.

"Good; then let's do that and be ready to go in about 15 minutes. I don't suppose this is going to settle?"

Both Taylor and Brent responded in the negative. The fight was on.

"Are there any issues you can stipulate to in order to save court time?"

"With all due respect, Your Honor, this is a capital case. I can't even stipulate as to the color of the sky," said Brent.

As he exited the Judge's chambers, Brent went into the corridor, waving to Sarah that he would be right back. He turned on his phone and impatiently waited for a cell.

Brent's first call was to Jack, which went instantly to his voice mail.

"Jack, it's Brent. Where the hell are you, man? The trial's started. Please call the office and check in with Melinda immediately."

His second call was to the office. Melinda had not heard from Jack at all. Brent gave her the most important task of her day: to find Jack.

"Call everyone on the contacts list who knows him. And call all the hospitals in the area – see if he's shown up there."

Brent started to hang up, then hesitated. "And Mimi?"

"Yes, boss?"

"Call the morgue."

CHAPTER TWENTY FOUR

"All rise!" called the Clerk. The buzz of the crowd instantly fell silent and everyone stood up as the judge entered the courtroom.

"The Superior Court for the State of California for the County of Los Angeles is now in session; the Honorable Adam Schwartz, Judge, presiding."

"Good morning ladies and gentlemen," said the judge. "Please be seated. We are on the record today in the case of *People v. Thomas.* Counsel, please state your appearances."

Brent and Taylor both stood up.

"Good morning, Your Honor. Brent Marks for the Defendant, William Thomas, who is

151

present in court." William stood next to Brent at the counsel table.

"Good morning, Your Honor. Benjamin Taylor for the people."

"Thank you, gentlemen. The record will reflect that counsel and the Court have conferred in chambers. Madame Clerk, please call in the first jury panel."

The Bailiff opened the door and both Taylor and Brent stood up again as an assortment of people began to file in and take seats in a section of the gallery that had been reserved for them. The Clerk had given an informational sheet to both Brent and Taylor regarding the identity of all the prospective jurors in the panel. As they took their seats, Brent looked at each one. There was not one black face in the bunch. As Brent sat down, William whispered, "How am I going to get a trial by my peers without any peers?"

"You knew the jury would most likely be white, William."

"Yeah, but I didn't know there'd be no blacks for him to kick off the jury."

Judge Schwartz gave the jury panel introductory instructions about the trial, what it was about, and the jury selection process. He made inquiries to eliminate people who were somehow connected to William, Brent, Taylor or Albright. At the judge's instruction, the Clerk then called the first twelve names at random, and the potential jurors were instructed to sit in the jury box for the voir *dire* process of jury qualification.

Benjamin Taylor had the first bite at the panel. Brent could see that he already seemed to be pleased with the color composition of the jury. It appeared to Brent that Taylor thought his job was already half over. Taylor posed his questions in a way which he hoped would educate the entire jury panel. Since his case, like most prosecutions, was not based on direct evidence, he explained the concept of circumstantial evidence and asked the jurors if they could be comfortable deciding William's fate based on a collection of circumstantial evidence that they would construct to put together like a puzzle of what really happened that night. All of the jurors seemed to understand this and were fine with it.

Then he explained that this was a capital case, in order to ascertain if anyone in the panel would be averse to making a decision on the guilt of the defendant knowing he could be sentenced to death in a later penalty phase of the trial. Only one of them seemed to be adverse to that: Virginia Knight, a 72-year-old retiree from the telephone company. Even those who professed to be devout Christians were comfortable with the idea, which gave William a chill down his spine.

Taylor continued his questioning; and with it, continued to seed the jury with elements of his case – a kind of legal brainwashing. When he was finally done, the judge kicked back into his role.

"Mr. Taylor, do you have any challenges for cause?"

"Pass for cause, Your Honor."

"Mr. Marks?"

"Pass for cause."

"Very well," said the judge. "The first peremptory challenge is with the People."

"The People would like to thank and excuse Mrs. Virginia Knight," said Taylor, as he kicked off the lady from the phone company who didn't feel right about the death penalty.

"Wonderful," whispered William to Brent.

"It's a long process, William. And, remember, they're watching your every move; so don't be so negative."

Brent knew that even though the judge would charge the jury that they should listen to all the evidence before they made up their minds, the chances were likely that 100% of them would have already decided if William was guilty or not sometime before the trial was over, and probably in its early stages.

* * *

After school, Dale Felder mostly wanted to hang out with his friends; but before that, he always had to do his dreaded chores. Cleaning up his room was the one task that ranked up there with doing his homework, so he opted for the low-lying fruit. He took out the trash. As he swung the garbage bag into the container in the alley, he saw what looked like a human hand protruding from behind it. Upon closer inspection, what Dale saw horrified him. He ran into the house screaming.

"Mom! Mom! There's a man out in the alley, and I think he's dead!"

CHAPTER TWENTY FIVE

When it was Brent's first turn to speak to the jurors, his initial questioning centered on the concept of reasonable doubt and that they had to presume William to be innocent unless the D.A. proved every element of the crime beyond a reasonable doubt. This was a difficult idea for Brent, who had a legal education and background, to convey to twelve people with no legal background whatsoever.

"Juror number three," he asked a 30-year-old female customer service representative from Department of Water and Power. "Do you understand that the defendant is presumed innocent?"

"Yes."

"Do you think you can set aside the natural human tendency of being suspicious of someone accused of a crime and treat him as innocent, unless the prosecution proves every element of murder beyond a reasonable doubt?"

"Yes."

People tended to regard lawyers as sneaky and manipulative. Brent's job during the trial would be to poke holes in each and every piece of the prosecution's evidence in order to plant the seed of reasonable doubt in the minds of the jurors but, at the same time, not look like he was trying to be tricky or deceitful.

Brent explained that the defense did not have to put on a case at all. It was all up to the prosecution, who had the entire burden of proving every element of the crime beyond a reasonable doubt. He described the concept of circumstantial evidence as if it were an ugly disease, and continued to question the jurors at length, exercising his peremptory challenges whenever he could spot an inkling of prejudice and praying for a person of color on the next jury panel.

* * *

At the end of the first day of trial a jury had not yet been selected, and Brent had not heard from Jack. His worry had evolved into distress. Not satisfied with Melinda's efforts alone, Brent called every hospital in the Los Angeles area for news of Jack and left his number with every one of them, not knowing if anyone would call back or not. Before leaving the courthouse, he stopped by the local police station (located in the complex) and put out a missing person report on Jack. He spent too much precious time at the police station, but it had to be done.

He then set up shop at the local Starbucks, going over Jack's reports for any clue of his whereabouts. It was a little hard to concentrate because of the music and the baristas constantly calling out names between the steaming musical pipes of the espresso machines. But the coffee smell was pleasant, it had a bathroom and free Wi-Fi, and it allowed Brent to be mobile; kind of like Charles Stinson's 'bare rear end' office.

After darkness fell, Brent hit the streets and cruised the working girls, showing them each a picture of Jack; but none of them recognized him – or they weren't talking. Taking the opportunity, he also showed them a photo of Albright. Finally he hit pay dirt (not the one he expected) from a pretty young African American prostitute who looked to be no more than 18, whom he had lured into his car with the prospect of offering her a trick.

"Don't know that one; but this one I do – yes, yes." She stabbed at the photo and looked up at Brent with her blue shadowed eyes.

"Who is he?"

"That's John. He's a scary son of a bitch, that one. I stay far away from him."

"Why?"

"He beat up my girlfriend really bad. Put her in the hospital."

Brent scribbled her name, Daisy McGovern, along with every phone number and address he was able to squeeze out of her, and even took a picture of her with his iPhone.

* * *

Brent made notes during his investigation, but although he had unexpectedly uncovered a lead in the case, he was no closer to finding Jack, which was his primary goal. Finally, after midnight, he gave up. The trial took priority over everything, even his missing friend. It was too late to go home, so Brent checked in to a local hotel and called Angela to ask her to take care of the cat.

At about three in the morning, Brent's phone rang. He groped for it on the nightstand like a blind man.

"Mr. Marks?"

"Yes," Brent said, opening his pasty eyes.

"This is Mary Priest from Presbyterian Hospital. I'm sorry to bother you at this hour, but you left a note to call you at any time, day or night."

"That's fine, fine. Is it about Jack Ruder?"

"Yes, sir. He's here with us, in intensive care. Does he have any family?"

"No, I'm the closest."

"In that case, could you come down in the morning, please?"

"Sure, sure. I've got a trial, but I could stop by before. What's his condition?"

"He's in critical condition, sir."

"Is he conscious?"

"No."

"Is he…"

161

"Sir, I'm just the night nurse. You'll have to discuss the particulars with his doctor."

"Of course. Court starts at nine. I can be there before eight."

"That will be fine."

CHAPTER TWENTY SIX

What little sleep Brent did get was broken by worries of Jack. Dreams about Jack dominated his light sleep and he could never be sure whether he was asleep or awake until the alarm on his cell phone went off at 6:00 a.m. Thankfully, the day would be reserved for choosing a jury; otherwise it would be impossible for Brent to survive the combat of trial. Brent gathered his trial notebooks and files and left the key in the hotel room as he took off early for the hospital so he could try to grab a quick breakfast later on the way to court.

Jack lay in a bed in the intensive care unit, hooked up to monitors and life support systems. They allowed Brent to go in and visit him for a moment, but Brent was not even sure whether

Jack was aware of his presence. It seemed as if he was in a coma, and he looked very beat up.

"You're going to get better, buddy, and then we'll find out who did this together," Brent said to Jack as he touched his shoulder.

"Does anyone know what happened to him?" he asked the nurse.

"A kid found him among the garbage cans in an alley. He's been pretty badly beaten."

"Can I see his records?"

"I'm afraid I can't let anyone but his closest relatives see them."

"He doesn't have any relatives. Not alive, anyway. He's my friend and my investigator. We were working on a case together, and I'm sure that's why this happened."

"I'm sorry, sir."

"Then, can I speak to his doctor?"

"Dr. Liu isn't in yet. He's due at 9 o'clock."

"I'll be in court at 9. When does he take his lunch break?"

"Usually around 1."

"Court breaks from 12 to 1:30. Tell him I'll be here at 12. Were the police called on this?"

"Yes."

Brent left a message for his secretary, to prepare and have served on the hospital a subpoena for all Jack's medical records and personal effects and to also obtain the police reports.

* * *

Brent paid for the deficit of sleep with a lack of sharpness at the trial. Having to take on the role of his missing investigator, who was on a valuable lead that could aid William's defense, was something that had to be dealt with. Jack was obviously onto something, and that was the reason he had ended up in the hospital. *But what was it?* For now, Brent had to divert his mind from that question and focus on trying to pick a jury that wouldn't decide against his client in the first minutes of the trial.

As jury selection continued, Brent asked questions of the prospective jurors based on current events in the post-September 11th world. The War on Terror, in Brent's opinion, had created a trend in American society to tolerate more interference by the police in exchange for a promise of physical safety. His interrogation ventured into that arena.

"Can I see a show of hands from the panel, please? How many of you have been stopped by police at a traffic stop?"

Nearly every hand went up.

"How many of you believe that, at a traffic stop, you must follow the commands of a police officer without question?"

Brent made a note of the three hands that went up to exercise his peremptory challenges.

"How many of you believe that the police treat African Americans differently than Caucasians?"

There was one hand from a young man who worked at the GM plant, which Brent noted.

"How many believe that the police should treat African Americans differently than Caucasians?"

There were no hands: an obvious product of "political correctness." Brent zeroed in, one by one, on the potential jurors who had shown their hands.

"Prospective Juror No. 4, Mr. Brandon: why do you believe that you must obey an officer's commands without question?"

"Because, the police are there to keep us safe."

"If the judge instructs you that you need not obey a police officer's commands if the police officer is acting illegally, would that change your mind about blind obedience?"

"Objection," said Taylor. "No such instruction has been agreed upon."

"It's true we haven't discussed instructions, but this is voir dire. I will allow it," said the Judge.

"I just think, in general, that it's not a wise decision to argue with someone who has authority over you. And it's even worse to argue with someone who has a gun."

There was some laughter among the gallery as Brent continued.

"How many of you are aware of the shooting of Michael Brown in Missouri?"

Half of the panel raised their hands.

"And how many of you think that the officer in that case was justified in shooting Michael Brown?"

Three hands shot up and Brent noted them. At this rate, he would exhaust his 20 challenges faster than he had anticipated. As the questioning continued, both Taylor and Brent alternatively evicted their least favorites from the jury panel, and the seats were filled by more undesirable candidates; kind of like a presidential election. The lack of African Americans on the panel made Brent sway towards trying to keep as many women on the jury as possible.

Finally, by the end of the day, neither side had any more challenges to make and, as a result, a jury of seven white women and five white men was sworn in. William's peers were ready to sit in judgment.

CHAPTER TWENTY SEVEN

Brent took an early dinner after court and drove home to grab several fresh changes of clothes. His night detective work required him to cut out the commute to and from Santa Barbara. Opening statements started tomorrow, and there would be no time to wait for the subpoenaed records and police reports. He needed answers and he needed them now.

It was already dark by the time Brent checked in to his new home away from home and went about the business of sleuthing. Charlotte Rutherford (aka 'Trixy') had not shown up in response to her subpoena, so Brent had to assume that either Jack didn't get a chance to serve her or that she just ignored it. Either way, she was his starting point.

Using the notes that Jack provided him, Brent bothered every one of the Starlight Motel residents; but none of them turned out to be Trixy and, of course, none of them had anything to say. He canvassed every hooker motel in the area, feeling more like a door-to-door salesman for an adult book store or a porno casting agent than an investigator. He expanded his investigation to local residences in the vicinity in order to determine where Jack had been at the time of the attack.

Conducting an investigation is like a series of job interviews. Getting the door slammed in your face at every attempt wasn't the exciting life of the detective portrayed on film or television. Brent wondered why Jack liked it so much. He looked at his watch – eleven p.m. *Kind of late to be knocking on doors – one more.*

Brent rapped on the door and the porch light came on.

"Who is it?" said the muffled male voice on the other side of the door.

"Brent Marks. I'm investigating a murder."

"Put your badge up where I can see it."

"I'm a lawyer. Here's my bar card," said Brent, holding up his ID

The door opened and a middle-aged man in blue jeans and a white T-shirt stood in the doorway with one hand on the door and the other in his pocket.

"It's pretty late," he said.

"I'm sorry, sir, but it's very important. My investigator was beaten pretty badly in this area and he's in a coma. I'm trying to…"

"Yeah, yeah, my son found him out back, in the alley."

"Your son? May I speak to him?"

"He's supposed to be getting ready for bed, but I'm sure he's still playing video games. Come on in."

Brent entered the humble residence, which was old but clean and smelled like an old book.

"Have a seat."

Brent sat down at a built-in table between the kitchen and living room. The kitchen light was on, but the living room was dark, illuminated by the glow of the eleven o'clock news. A plump woman in a bathrobe came up to Brent.

"Hello. Can I get you something to drink?"

"Hello, ma'am. Yes, water would be great."

The lady got a plastic cup out of the closet, filled it with tap water, and held it out to Brent.

"Here you go."

The man returned with a teenaged boy who was wearing shorts and a T-shirt and had his head bowed in reverence to his iPhone, his eyes glued to the screen and his fingers clicking away.

"Put that thing down," said the man. "This is Mr…?"

"Marks. Brent Marks."

"Mr. Marks wants to talk to you about the guy you found out back in the alley."

The boy, Jason Tremble, reluctantly slipped his phone into his pocket with a look of impatience and sat down next to Brent at the kitchen counter table. He looked up at Brent with curious, chocolate eyes.

"You a cop?"

"No, I'm a lawyer. The man you found was my investigator. Can you tell me about it?"

The boy recounted how he had found Jack in the alley among the trash cans behind his house, but he didn't see anything other than Jack, and he didn't hear anything, because he had just come from inside to take out the garbage. Brent thanked the family, left, and went behind their house to the alley. A couple of cats darted away as he approached; one jumping over a wall and the other ducking behind an old TV stand that had been put out to pasture. As he stood there looking at a hodgepodge of plastic and metal garbage cans in the crisp cold air, which smelled like dead fish, he asked out loud: "*What were you doing here, buddy?*"

CHAPTER TWENTY EIGHT

The first order of business in the trial was the attorneys' opening statements. This would be the only time the lawyers had a chance to speak to the jury directly before the end of the trial, when they would give their closing arguments. For the opening statements, they were not allowed to argue their position; only summarize what they expected the witnesses and the physical evidence to present during the trial.

A trial is an infallible process. It has often been described as a way to find the truth; but in reality, that was an impossibility. The truth is not contained within the fingerprints on a gun or even the memory of an eyewitness. Memories are not recordings stored in your head. They are constructed from many parts of the brain, and even recalling the simplest thing is a complex task for it to do.

Because of the brain's tendency to create, organize, and make sense of things, the imagination often plays a part in memory, with the brain filling in the "blanks" of a particular memory with facts that make sense, but may not necessarily have happened. That is why three people who witnessed the same thing will tell three very convincing but very different stories. It doesn't make the memory any less real, and people are usually convinced of their brain's version of the story.

A trial is kind of like a TV game show where the contestants, or witnesses, tell their stories and a group of judges decide who wins and who gets "kicked out." As imperfect as it was, this was the game show that would decide the fate of William Thomas.

Benjamin Taylor had the honor of having the first and the last word in the trial, so he took the lectern in front of the jury box first to begin his statement. Taylor was handsomely dressed in a grey suit with a light blue shirt and dark blue tie. He delivered his speech with the confidence and style of a first-rate orator, without legalese and in a manner calculated to implant an outline in the jury's collective head of his version of the case.

The old adage "You never get a second chance to make a first impression" is true in a jury trial over anything else. Taylor put on his best genuine smile when he took the podium and looked eye-to-eye with each and every juror as he made his speech. This would be the first time they would hear about the facts of the case, and he aimed to indelibly burn his version into their skulls.

"Ladies and gentlemen of the jury: this is a very simple case. You will hear Officer John Albright testify that he and his partner, David Shermer, stopped the defendant's car late at night on Burbank Boulevard due to suspicious and possibly criminal activity. The defendant's two companions were detained for urinating in public and the defendant was detained due to having an open container of alcohol in his car, and suspicion of driving under the influence of alcohol.

"Officer Albright will testify that during the routine field tests he attempted to administer to the defendant to determine if he was, indeed, under the influence of alcohol, the defendant became belligerent and refused to follow instructions. Then the defendant attempted to take Officer Albright's baton, which posed a risk to the officer's safety and the safety of his partner. Officer Albright succeeded in getting the baton back and, for his safety and the safety of Officer Shermer, he struck the defendant in the knee with his baton to avoid a further violent confrontation.

"But this was not enough for the defendant; no!"

"Objection, Your Honor: counsel is arguing."

It was a risk Brent took, making an objection during an opening statement, as the jury could get the impression he was being sneaky or unfair and trying to interrupt his opponent's train of thought.

"Sustained. The jury will disregard the last sentence of the People's opening statement."

The risk paid off. Of course, the jury couldn't erase what they heard, but they knew that Taylor had ventured out of bounds. They just didn't know why.

Taylor, undaunted, continued: "Officer Albright will testify that the defendant continued to struggle with the officer's attempts to subdue him and, in the struggle, the defendant attempted to (and did) put his hands on Officer Albright's pistol, and fired it, resulting in the death of Officer Shermer."

The men and women of the jury were alert and taking notes as Taylor continued his statement.

"The People will call a fingerprint expert, who will testify that the defendant's fingerprints were on Officer Albright's gun. We will further call a weapons expert who will testify that, in his expert opinion, Officer Albright's gun had been tampered with."

Taylor went on to tell the jury, in a very simple way, what evidence he intended to present; as if he were telling the jury a story. He concluded his statement with: "After you have heard all the evidence here in court that I have just described to you, the People are going to ask you to render your verdict that William Thomas..." Taylor paused and pointed an accusatory finger at William "William Thomas, the defendant, is guilty of capital murder."

As much as Brent didn't want Taylor's opening statement to sit and gel in the jurors' minds for an hour and a half during the break without a rebuttal from him, Taylor had calculated his speech to end exactly at 12 p.m., and the Court recessed for lunch. Even though they were cautioned that an opening statement was not evidence, Brent fully expected that Taylor's words would become petrified in the jurors' minds, and he would have the arduous task of convincing them that William was not guilty. Law or no law, the burden of proof, which once had rested on the People, had shifted to the Defendant.

* * *

After the lunch break was over and everyone had returned to Court, Brent was invited to the podium to give his presentation. He stood there at the lectern, looking at the jury, and kept his eyes focused on them during the entire speech. He was dressed in a navy blue suit with a teleprompter blue shirt and dark blue tie. It looked as if he and Taylor had been dressed by the same mother.

"Ladies and Gentlemen, I represent the defendant, William Thomas. As you've all been instructed by the judge: neither I nor Mr. Thomas has to prove anything to you in this case. The People have the sole burden to convince you, beyond a reasonable doubt, of every element of the crime of which my client stands accused.

"That means that Mr. Thomas does not have to *say anything* or do *anything* in his defense. The entire case rests upon the quality, or lack thereof, of the evidence that the People present. You shouldn't expect myself or Mr. Thomas to explain anything about the evidence. You and you alone bear the burden of weighing and examining each and every piece of evidence and all the witnesses' testimony to decide if it supports every element of the crime of capital murder.

"I disagree with Mr. Taylor that this is a simple case. It's a very difficult case, and your job is the most difficult of any of us in this room. You've all heard that there are two sides to every story. Well, given the infallible nature of human beings, there may be many, many sides to the same story. People have different perceptions of what they have seen or heard, and the physical evidence may lead to many different conclusions or inferences.

"The judge will instruct you that William Thomas was not obliged to follow every instruction of John Albright with a smile on his face. The law says that if a police officer is acting illegally, you don't have to blindly do what he says.

"You will hear evidence from a firearms and ballistics expert, called by the defense, that it is not possible from an examination of the gun to determine who shot the fatal shot that killed David Shermer. You will hear the People's own fingerprint expert testify that it is impossible to determine from the fingerprints whether John Albright or William Thomas pulled the trigger. You will hear the testimony of an accident reconstruction expert, who will conclude that Officer Albright's version of the struggle with

Mr. Thomas could not have happened the way he will say it did.

"You will hear the testimony of William's two friends, eyewitnesses who were passengers in his car, who will testify that William was already on the ground and that Officer Albright was sitting on top of his chest when he pulled his weapon out, pointed it at William's face, and said: 'Nigger, your momma is not going to recognize you at your funeral.'

"Finally, you will hear the testimony of an expert who will show you an enhanced video of portions of the incident, and you will clearly see from the video that, at the time Albright pulled his gun and pointed it at William, his handcuffs were still locked away in his belt.

"After hearing and considering all of this evidence, ladies and gentlemen, I am confident that you will find that the People cannot prove every element of capital murder against William beyond a reasonable doubt; which means that, under the law, you must acquit him."

CHAPTER TWENTY NINE

It was the first day of testimony, and Brent had a client with no memory, a hot lead gone cold due to an unconscious investigator, a tough-on-crime judge, and a prosecutor bent on sending William to death row to achieve his political aspirations. The odds seemed better in Las Vegas.

Benjamin Taylor put his strongest foot forward and called Detective Daniel Salerno as his first witness, who expertly described the physical evidence found at the scene. Dressed in classic beige slacks and a brown blazer, Detective Salerno had a no-nonsense, professional air about him. He was straight out of an episode of Law & Order, and spoke to the jury with the skill of a professional storyteller, training his grey eyes on them as he testified.

Taylor was smart to put on the strongest part of his case (and the best witnesses) while the members of the jury were still paying half attention to what was going on in court and less of what was on their grocery shopping lists, how their favorite ball teams were doing, what shows they were missing on TV, or what was going on at work. They could focus their thinking on these more important subjects when they had already made up their minds whether William was guilty or not, which would probably be about halfway through the case, if not sooner.

As the first detective to arrive that night, Salerno described a crime scene professionally secured, the careful retrieval of Officer Albright's gun (which he had personally found in the bushes), and the state of inebriation of TJ and Fenton, who had blood alcohol levels of .16 and .18, respectively and had both pleaded guilty to charges of being drunk in public as well as public urination. In the first hour of testimony of the first prosecution witness, Brent's only eyewitnesses had been sufficiently discredited.

"Detective Salerno, you understand the distinction between 'under the influence of alcohol' and 'drunk,' do you not?" Taylor postulated.

"Objection: calls for a legal conclusion," Brent interjected.

"Overruled: this witness has been qualified as an expert. Please answer the question."

"I do."

"Please explain your understanding of the difference."

"'Under the influence of alcohol' is a term used to describe the state of being after a subject has consumed enough alcohol to alter his judgment and motor skills so that operating a motor vehicle or machinery would be unsafe to himself and possibly others.

"'Drunk' is the state of intoxication which includes 'under the influence,' but goes further. It is the state of intoxication in which one loses control of one's faculties and behavior."

"As a result of your interview of Timothy Jones, how would you describe his condition?"

"Objection: lack of foundation."

"Overruled."

"Mr. Jones was drunk."

"And upon which facts do you support that opinion?"

"My observation of his physical condition. He was unsteady on his feet, his eyes were watery and bloodshot, his speech was slurred, and he had a hard time keeping his balance when he spoke to me."

Brent noted two women on the jury who could not hide their expressions of disgust and kicked himself for not using some of his peremptory challenges to kick off the teetotalers. That would cost him, and cost William.

"As a result of your interview of Fenton Washington, can you describe his condition?"

"Mr. Washington was also drunk."

In Taylor's trademark move of allowing the jury the lunch hour for all the damaging information to set in, he did not finish with Salerno until 11:58, and court recessed two minutes early.

* * *

Salerno continued to testify after the break, carefully identifying every report and every piece of physical evidence. He testified as to the proper safekeeping and cataloging of every scrap of physical evidence found on the scene, including the opened can of beer found in William's car and the car itself. Defense attorneys often argue that evidence could have possibly been tainted because the police cannot account for its custody from the scene of the crime until the trial. That was not going to happen in this case.

Brent had few questions for Salerno on cross-examination. He simply did not want to reiterate the fallibility of his two main witnesses, which Taylor would surely emphasize on redirect. Instead, he ventured into an area that was not covered in Salerno's testimony.

"Detective Salerno, does the Los Angeles Police Department have a "Use of Force Review Division"?"

"Objection! Outside the scope of direct," barked Taylor.

"It is outside the scope, Mr. Marks."

"Yes, Your Honor. I can either recall Detective Salerno as an adverse witness or simply wrap it up now to save time."

That lit a fire in Judge Schwartz's heart. He loved the idea of saving court time.

"Overruled. Please proceed, Mr. Marks."

"Thank you, Your Honor.

"Yes, there is a "Use of Force Review Division"."

"And what is the purpose of that division?"

"Its purpose is to examine and analyze the lethal, non-lethal and less-lethal force used by LAPD officers throughout the year and provide an overview of their investigation."

"And do they issue periodic reports on their findings?"

"Yes, they do."

"Are you familiar with these reports?"

"Yes, I am."

Brent asked the Clerk for Officer Albright's firearm, which he carefully took from her, making eye contact from the gun to the jury and back on the gun again. He stood in the well in front of the witness box, holding the weapon in his hand as if it would go off by itself.

"This is a very dangerous instrument, isn't it, Detective Salerno?"

"Yes, it is."

"This is an 8045F .45 caliber Beretta, isn't it?"

"Yes, it is."

"Do you know the capacities of this pistol, Detective?"

"I am familiar with them, yes."

"Objection, Your Honor.   The capacities of the pistol are irrelevant."

"Your Honor, how could the capacities of the instrument of death in this case be irrelevant?"

"Approach the bench, please."

Brent, Taylor, and the judge huddled at the bench to discuss the objection.

"What is the relevance of this line of questioning, Mr. Marks?"

"Your Honor, these are foundational questions which I will connect with the policies of the LAPD for the use of force, including firearms such as this."

"This is a capital case, so I'll allow this line of questioning. But please connect it up before we lose the jury."

"Yes, Your Honor."

Back at counsel table, Brent restated the last question, and Salerno answered, "This is a recoil-operated, locked breech semi-automatic pistol."

"By semi-automatic, it is capable of firing more than one round in rapid succession, is that correct?"

"Yes."

"Given that kind of power, wouldn't you agree that the only purpose for using a weapon like this is to kill?"

"Objection, Your Honor: argumentative!"

"Certainly discharging a weapon such as this in the presence of other people is likely to kill or injure someone, Your Honor."

"Overruled."

"The purpose of using a weapon like this is to inflict grave bodily harm or kill to protect the officer, other police officers, or the public."

Salerno knew which side he was on, but he could not hide the respect he had for the weapon.

"Are there policies in effect at the LAPD regarding the use of firearms such as this?"

"Yes."

"And you are familiar with these policies, correct?"

"Of course."

"In fact, every officer in the LAPD is trained on these policies, isn't that correct?"

"Yes."

"And these policies are contained in a manual that every officer is issued, isn't that correct?"

190

"Yes."

"Am I correctly stating this policy: 'that personnel may only use that force which is "objectively reasonable" to defend themselves, defend others, to effect an arrest or detention, to prevent escape, or to overcome resistance?"

"Yes."

"And an officer is authorized to use deadly force only to protect himself or others from an immediate threat of death or serious bodily injury, to prevent a crime where the suspect's actions place persons in jeopardy of death or serious bodily injury, or to apprehend a fleeing felon for a crime involving serious bodily injury or where there is a substantial risk that the suspect will cause death or serious bodily injury to others if he or she is not quickly apprehended?"

"That sounds correct."

"The very act of drawing a weapon is the use of deadly force, isn't it, Detective?"

"Objection: argumentative!"

"I'm asking for an expert opinion, Your Honor, within the confines of LAPD policy."

"Overruled. The witness may answer if he has an opinion."

"When an officer draws his weapon, that is an exercise of deadly force, isn't it, Detective?"

Salerno hesitated. He knew where Brent was going, but he was up against the wall and had to answer honestly.

"Yes."

"In fact, by definition, the manual says that the use of a weapon constitutes deadly force, correct?"

"That is correct."

"And, pursuant to the policy of the LAPD, an officer should only use deadly force if he has no other clear alternative; isn't that correct?"

"Yes, it is."

CHAPTER THIRTY

Brent couldn't rely on just his cross-examination skills to blow a cloud of reasonable doubt in front of the jury like some kind of judicial magic trick. He needed to find out what Jack had been working on; and quickly.

He started, as usual, at the hospital, where Jack's condition was about the same; although his vitals had improved a little. Jack's personal effects, his wallet, his phone, and everything else had not been on his person when he was found. It appeared as if he had been robbed. His attending physician, Dr. Gregorian, was encouraging about Jack's condition. "Usually, and we don't know why it is, the systems just come back online and the patient just wakes up."

"Just like that?"

"Just like that. And all we do is keep them alive and just wait."

Brent talked to the motionless, slumbering Jack about the case. *Maybe he'll decide to wake up and help me before it's too late.* After about half an hour, Brent decided to give up on waiting for Jack (at least for the time being) and ventured out into the underworld to work Jack's case – their case.

Brent located Daisy easily this time and took her for dinner at a local Chili's. As Daisy wolfed down a rack of ribs and fries and a bathtub-sized blended Margarita, she brought Brent up to date on what was being said on the streets.

"I hear that there's a group of cops who have taken over running the girls around here."

"Including you?"

"Nope, I'm independent."

"Self-employed."

"You got it. But they ran my girlfriend, Tiffany. That's how she got all messed up."

"Which, I suppose, is also the reason you remained self-employed."

"You're smart. You a lawyer or something?"

"Very funny, Daisy. Seriously," Brent asked, stirring his cup of coffee with milk, "don't you ever think about going home? You don't seem to me like the kind of girl who agrees with life on the streets."

"I'm never, ever going back there!"

"Evil stepmother?"

"Evil stepfather. With nasty thoughts and nastier hands. I decided that if I was gonna be treated like a piece of meat, I was going to charge for it."

Daisy finished her ribs and ordered a quesadilla and another double Margarita. At this rate, by the time she reached her 21st birthday, she wouldn't need to go out drinking.

"You'll probably be glad to know that I think I found your Trixy," she finally said. "They moved her out to Studio City to work Ventura Boulevard. You should find her there most nights."

Brent thanked Daisy for the leads, paid the bill, took her back to Sepulveda, and dropped her off. Then he went out to seek the elusive Trixy.

The waiting paid off a little after midnight. Brent spotted a girl exiting a white Mustang at a Shell station. The Mustang drove away and the girl went inside to buy a pack of cigarettes. As she exited and headed down the boulevard, she passed right by Brent's car, and he knew for sure that it was her. He rolled down his window and she took the bait.

"Hi Honey, wanna date?" she asked, as she approached the car. "Oh, it's you! Get away from me. If they see me with you, I'll be in deep shit," she said as she pushed away from the window and broke into a trot.

Brent jumped out of the car and followed, walking quickly to try to keep her pace. She turned around and yelled: "Quit following me – you'll be sorry!"

Ignoring her, Brent continued and picked up the chase. When he was close enough behind her to smell her perfume, he reached out and grabbed her by the elbow.

"Let go of me!" she cried.

"Calm down. I just want to talk to you."

"You're such an asshole. Don't you get it?"

Suddenly, a black and white patrol car pulled up, windows open.

"This man bothering you, ma'am?" asked a young policeman.

Trixy looked nervous. Maybe it was because she was afraid of being arrested for prostitution. Maybe something more.

"No, no, I'm fine. It was just a mistake."

"Why don't you step in the car, ma'am? You'll be safe with us."

Somehow it didn't appear that Trixy was buying that.

"I told you, sir," she said to Brent. "I don't know anything about your sister. You've mistaken me for someone else."

"I'm sorry to bother you, Miss. Officers, this is all a big misunderstanding."

"We'll see about that. Let me see your driver's license, sir," said the young blond cop, as he stepped out of the car.

Brent pulled out his wallet and gave his license to the officer.

"You looking for a date tonight?" he asked.

"No, no. It was just a misunderstanding. I thought I knew that girl."

"This is a heavy area for prostitution. Stay right here while my partner checks on some things," he said as he handed Brent's ID to the driver of the police car.

After about half an hour, the police let Brent go. He was happy not to be spending the night in some holding cell somewhere, and decided to call it a night.

CHAPTER THIRTY ONE

On the second day of Taylor's case-in-chief, Brent still had not excused Detective Salerno. He was on a roll – an unreasonable force roll. Salerno took the stand. The jurors were all buzzed up on coffee and their eyes were open. If Brent was lucky, he would be able to monopolize the morning and Taylor would be doing his redirect of Salerno in front of twelve hungry, droopy-eyed, sleepy people who were thinking about dinner or calling home – anything but the trial.

"Detective Salerno, according to LAPD policy, an officer has several types of force available to him, in varying degrees according to the particular situation; isn't that true?"

"Yes."

"He can use verbalization. In other words, give the suspect a command, correct?"

"That's correct."

"Or he can use bodily force, like the application of body weight, take downs, wrist locks, strikes, kicks and punches, correct?"

"Yes."

"In fact, that is the force you observed Officer Albright using in the video before he pulled his gun, isn't that correct?"

"Yes, he was using his body weight to subdue the suspect."

Taylor was anxious, like a dog waiting for the food bowl to be placed on the ground, or a caged wild animal. But Brent still had the floor.

"An officer also can use OC spray, or pepper spray, correct?"

"Yes."

"Or a Taser, which completely incapacitates the suspect; isn't that correct?"

"If done properly, yes."

"Was Officer Albright's Taser one of the items of evidence seized from the scene?"

"Yes, it was."

"And was it fully charged and in good working order at the time of seizure?"

"Yes."

"Yet he chose not to use it."

"Objection! Calls for speculation and is argumentative!"

"Sustained. The jury will disregard the question."

Too late. It was the most interesting thing they have heard so far. Bring it home, Brent.

"And Officer Albright also had the option to use an impact device, such as his baton, correct?"

"Yes."

"And he already, in fact, used his baton, correct?"

"Yes."

"Yet, at the point where Officer Albright had his body weight applied to the body of Mr. Thomas, he chose to use deadly force by withdrawing his pistol, isn't that correct?"

"Objection! Argumentative!"

"Sustained. The jury is cautioned to disregard the question."

"No further questions, Your Honor."

"Redirect?"

"Thank you, Your Honor," said Taylor, as he finally got the chance to rehabilitate his witness.

"Detective Salerno, an officer's choice of what type of force to use is determined by the circumstances of the situation, isn't it?"

"Objection: leading!"

"Overruled. It's foundational. The witness may answer."

"Yes, we cannot second guess or apply our judgment in hindsight to an officer who feels the need to protect himself or his partner from bodily injury."

Taylor elicited what LAPD policy allowed an officer to consider in choosing what type of force to apply. These factors included: whether the suspect is posing an immediate threat to the safety of the officer or others, whether the suspect is actively resisting arrest, the time available to make the decision, a reasonable officer's experience and training, and literally everything in the environment around the officer and suspect's immediate vicinity.

"Detective Salerno, in your opinion, given your examination of the reports and the facts and circumstances surrounding this incident, was it unreasonable for Officer Albright to pull his weapon?"

Brent couldn't object. He was the one who, with full judicial latitude, had used Salerno as an expert witness. Now came the blow that would have the effect of erasing or at least diminishing the impact of his entire line of cross-examination.

"I cannot say that it was unreasonable under the circumstances."

Taylor's circus was back on track, and he was again the ringmaster.

* * *

The Taylor show continued after the break with a video expert who played the first cut of the video that TJ had taken on the scene; first all the way through, then he walked the jury through individual frames he had blown up and enhanced to show that William had grabbed Officer Albright's gun. On cross-examination, Brent aimed to destroy the expert, a short, balding tech geek with goofy tortoiseshell glasses. He showed the jury a frame of the video that had been blown up, showing William and Albright struggling for the gun.

"Mr. Tanner, isn't it true in this blown-up frame you have identified – it is not possible to see whether Mr. Thomas or Officer Albright has control over the gun?"

"I wouldn't say it's impossible."

"Move to strike as non-responsive, Your Honor."

"Granted. Please answer the question."

"As it is framed, I cannot answer the question. Nothing is impossible."

Oh come on! Just answer the damn question!

"Move to strike, Your Honor."

"Granted."

"Mr. Tanner, can't you answer any question honestly?"

"Objection! Argumentative!" called Taylor, shooting a nasty glare at Brent.

"Sustained. The jury will disregard Mr. Marks's question."

"Mr. Tanner, looking at the frame you have blown up, you don't see anything that we don't see, isn't that correct?"

"Yes, I would say that that is correct."

Then just say it!

"To me, I just see a picture with two pairs of hands on one gun: a gun that is pointed directly at Mr. Thomas's face..."

"Objection, Your Honor: counsel's opinion is irrelevant and the question is argumentative."

"Withdraw the question, Your Honor."

"Sustained."

"You testified it was at this point in the video where my client took the gun away from Officer Albright. However, isn't it true that this frame you've blown up doesn't show the gun being wrenched from Albright's control? On the contrary, it shows it clearly that it did not leave his hands; isn't that correct?"

"Objection: compound."

"Overruled. You may answer the question."

"Well, that is subject to various interpretations."

"And your expertise is in video enhancement, not guns; isn't that correct?"

"Yes, but…"

"In fact, you don't own a handgun yourself, do you?"

"No, but…"

"So you're not qualified to express the opinion that the gun is being taken from Officer Albright in this frame, isn't that correct?"

"Objection! Argumentative!"

"Withdraw the question, Your Honor. Nothing further."

Taylor next called to the stand Joseph Stevens, a gun expert and retired LAPD patrolman. Stevens's qualifications as an expert were beyond reproach. He had spent many years reconstructing shootings and testifying, mostly on the plaintiff's side, and knew how to establish a rapport with the jury.

Stevens's show and tell was complete with blown up photographs of Albright's 8045F .45 caliber Beretta and he carefully demonstrated to the jury that the magazine and slide of the officer's pistol were damaged, indicating that the gun had been tampered with, which was not something a trained officer would do.

He also testified that the slide of the pistol had been partially engaged and a second round had been partially ejected and had fouled the firing chamber. It was his opinion that the gun had gone off after William had wrenched it out of Albright's hands. By the lunch break, the case was a hangman's noose which had had been tightly fastened around William's neck.

* * *

Brent attacked the prosecution's expert witness right after court was called to order.

"Mr. Stevens, isn't it correct that none of the physical evidence you described in your testimony can lead you to the conclusion that my client, William Thomas, was the one who fired the gun?"

"I'm not sure I understand the question. The gun appears to have been fired a first time during the struggle, and there was an attempt to fire it again."

"Move to strike as unresponsive, Your Honor."

When can one of you hired guns just answer a simple question?

"Granted. The jury will disregard the witness's answer. Mr. Stevens, you are to answer the question, sir."

"Sorry, Your Honor. Can you please repeat the question?"

Now he's hard of hearing.

"I'll rephrase it. In your examination of the gun, you cannot determine, beyond a reasonable doubt, whether Mr. Thomas fired it or whether Officer Albright shot it, isn't that correct?"

"The first time or the second time?"

"How about the first time?"

"No, I was not able to determine that the first time."

"And you were also not able to determine, beyond a reasonable doubt, whether Mr. Thomas or Officer Albright attempted to fire it the second time; isn't that correct?"

"I was not able to determine that, no."

"In fact, Mr. Stevens, isn't it true that both Mr. Thomas and Officer Albright could have simultaneously caused the gun to fire the first time?"

"I suppose that is possible."

"Move to strike as non-responsive, Your Honor."

"Granted."

"Yes or no, Mr. Stevens: isn't it true that both Mr. Thomas and Officer Albright could have simultaneously caused the gun to fire the first time?"

Stevens looked as if his temperature was being taken with a rectal thermometer.

"Yes," he said, reluctantly.

"No further questions."

Taylor let it stand, opting not to redirect. William leaned over to Brent and whispered, "Great job."

"Thanks, but this is just expert testimony. It still comes down to whether they believe you or Albright."

On re-direct, Taylor fought back.

"Mr. Stevens, in your original testimony yesterday, you didn't claim to know who actually shot the gun, did you?"

"No, I did not. I simply testified that the gun went off during the struggle, and it appeared that the chamber had been fouled because the firearm had been tampered with, which is something no trained police officer would do. That was the basis of my opinion that it was the defendant who shot the gun, not Officer Albright."

Brent tried to get Stevens to admit on re-cross that the gun could have gone off the first time because Albright had initiated the shot but William pushed the gun away. He tried to do this by posing a hypothetical question, which Stevens managed to weasel out of at every turn, so Brent finally gave up.

Taylor called a fingerprint expert, who testified that both William's and Albright's fingerprints were found on Officer Albright's gun.

"Cross-examination?"

"Thank you, Your Honor. Mr. Lebed, isn't it true that you were unable to lift any discernible fingerprints from the trigger of the weapon?"

"That is true."

"So, from the fingerprint evidence on the gun, it is not possible for you to opine that William Thomas fired the gun, isn't that correct?"

"But, his fingerprints were on the gun."

"Move to strike as non-responsive."

"Granted. The witness will answer the question."

"I'll repeat. You cannot say from the fingerprint evidence on the gun that William Thomas was the person who fired it, isn't that correct?"

"It was either the defendant who shot it or the officer shot his own partner, which is inconceivable."

"Move to strike again, Your Honor."

"Granted. Answer the question please, sir."

"Yes."

"Thank you, no further questions."

"Mr. Taylor, redirect?"

"Thank you, Your Honor. From the fingerprint evidence, can you give an opinion as to the person or persons who fired that weapon last?"

"Yes. It could have only been Mr. Thomas." A pause, then: "Or Officer Albright."

"Thank you, no further questions."

CHAPTER THIRTY TWO

While it was true that the trial was the most important thing in Brent's life at this particular moment in time, rest was also important. He could only do so much poking about in the lives of call girls looking for evidence of police corruption without Jack's help, and putting another investigator on at this point would be a waste of time. By the time he got up to speed, the trial would be over. Brent shoved his dirty laundry into his suitcase and headed for home for a few hours of rest and relaxation.

The first stop after the long drive to Santa Barbara was the office, which looked like an abandoned battle zone. There was a stack of mail that would not be reviewed until the end of the trial, piles of messages that would go unanswered, and all the remains of a law practice on hold. As Brent prepared to dive into the stack of papers to look for ones that may be relevant to the trial, he noticed a phone message that Melinda clearly marked "URGENT" with a huge yellow post-it note bigger than the message itself. Brent's cell phone rang.

"Boss, I've been trying to call you. I just left the office and got a call from the hospital."

"I'm at the office. I see your message here."

Jack had come out of his coma. It was time to go back to L.A.

* * *

Brent ran out of the office, jumped into his car, and headed home for a quick shower, change of clothes, a repack of his suitcase and the return trip to Los Angeles. When he reached home, the fresh air and the twinkling lights of the harbor beckoned him to stay, but that was not a choice that was available to him at that point. When he opened the door the cat ran out, then back in, almost tripping him as she scooted between his ankles. Her needs had to be satisfied first.

Brent raced Calico to the kitchen (she won) and he fixed her a bowl of cat food, which he tossed onto the floor. As she lapped up the food, Brent went to the bedroom, undressed and jumped in the shower.

When he exited the shower, standing completely naked in his bedroom and examining the contents of his closet for something to wear, he heard:

"My, my!"

Brent spun around, facing Angela, who stood in the doorway, smiling.

"What are you doing?" she asked innocently, batting her eyes and smiling as she leaned against the doorjamb, seductively.

How do they learn that; or are they just born with it?

The resistance of temptation was reaching a critical point for Brent. Home was truly the best place he could possibly be; but, alas, it was not an available option.

"Angie, I, um…"

"You have to go."

"Jack just woke up."

Angela's look switched from mischief to disappointment and then to business.

"I'll help you pack."

* * *

The haggard, peaked version of Jack was not the one that Brent was most used to; but it was far better than the ghost of Jack he had been visiting during the past several days. He still looked like he had been embalmed with whatever was responsible for the medicinal smell in his room. Jack was sleeping when Brent approached.

"You look great, buddy."

Jack's eyes opened, half-slits, and the corners of his mouth curved a little. His lips moved slightly and he whispered hoarsely, "Fuck you."

Brent smiled.

"Now, get your lazy ass out of that bed and get back to work. We have a trial to win."

Jack's eyebrows furrowed in a frown. Brent took the body language as a question.

"We're two days into Taylor's case-in-chief. Not getting slaughtered too badly, I guess. I've been spending the nights with your girlfriends on Sepulveda Boulevard."

Jack's monitors jumped. He looked scared, preoccupied. Brent leaned over the bed.

"You all right, Jack?"

"Don't go there," Jack whispered. "Too dangerous."

"Don't worry, Jack. I've kind of taken it as far as I could without your input. The way I figure it (and stop me if I'm wrong) is that these dirty cops are taking a piece of the prostitution trade, or a piece of the prostitutes, or both. Am I on the right track?"

Jack blinked in the affirmative.

"Do you know who the officers are?"

Their conversation, if you could call it that, was suddenly interrupted by a fat brunette nurse waving her arms and telling Brent he had overstayed his welcome and that Jack had to rest. Jack made a moaning sound, then mumbled something that sounded like numbers. Brent leaned in for better reception.

Jack whispered, and Brent caught the number 'fifteen.' Then a name, "Robert."

"Robert who?"

Jack strained in frustration. Fifteen again. Then Robert. Then seven.

"15-Robert-7?"

"Yes," Jack's throaty rasp confirmed. "Go to IAG."

CHAPTER THIRTY THREE

Officer John Albright had been well prepared for this moment. After all, a great deal depended on this trial; and not just William's life. Benjamin Taylor had invested his entire political career in it. Albright strode to his seat in the witness box with a self-assured gait and regarded the jury sincerely with confidence, yet exuded innocence. Hatless and dressed in a clean, perfectly ironed police uniform, his ivory skin and short, light brown hair was what the jury noticed before the badge. He was a grandson, a son, a brother. Taylor introduced Albright to the jury through direct examination as a highly respected, honored, and decorated officer who had achieved the status of enrollment in the elite Metro Division, the pinnacle of a brilliant law enforcement career.

"Officer Albright, can you please describe what happened on the night of October 7th of last year?"

"Yes. My partner, Officer David Shermer, and I were on patrol in the San Fernando Valley. At approximately 0100 hours, we spotted a late model blue Cadillac Escalade pulled over on the 15000 block of Burbank Boulevard, where two subjects outside the car were engaged in suspicious activity."

It was apparent to Brent that Taylor had prepared Albright well, but this didn't prevent him from sounding robotic, as most police officers do when they testify in court.

"What do you mean by 'suspicious activity'?"

"They were loitering. At that point what they were doing there at that hour was unknown to us, so we pulled behind the car, activated our red lights, and got out to investigate. There are a lot of stores and businesses in that neighborhood, including a gold broker, and it is known as a high crime area."

"What did you observe at that time?"

"Two African American males, approximately mid-30s, appeared to be intoxicated and urinating on the street, and one African American male remained in the car, apparently the driver."

"And what, if anything did you do at that point?"

"I contacted the driver, while Officer Shermer secured the other two suspects."

"Who was the driver?"

"Him. The defendant – William Thomas," said Albright, pointing an accusatory finger at William.

"Your Honor, may I request that the Court order the defendant to stand for identification, please?" asked Taylor.

"Objection. Highly prejudicial, Your Honor."

"Overruled. The defendant will please rise."

At six foot three, William towered over most of the men in the jury. *Is this a man you would want to meet in a dark alley?*

The jury knew full well who William was. Even so, the finger pointing got a rise out of them. Taylor was emphasizing William's size and girth more than anything else.

"What happened after your contact with the driver?"

"I asked for his license and registration. Officer Shermer then informed me that he had observed an open container of alcohol in plain view in the back of the vehicle. There was a smell of alcoholic beverages in the car and this led me to suspect the driver was possibly under the influence of alcohol."

"What did you do at that point?"

"I decided to run sobriety field tests on the defendant to ascertain if he was under the influence of alcohol."

Albright next described the various field tests that he intended to administer to William, including the finger to nose test and the heel to toe walking test, known in law enforcement circles as the "walk and turn field sobriety test."

"And what were the results of those tests?"

"I never had a chance to run them."

"Why not?"

"Because the defendant became belligerent, uncooperative and violent after I asked him to step out of the vehicle. Not only did he fail to follow instructions, but he took actions that put myself and my partner in serious jeopardy."

"What kinds of actions?"

"During the finger to nose field sobriety test, the defendant became unruly and interrupted the test, insisting that he was not drunk. I then instructed him on the walk and turn field sobriety test, which he refused to perform. When he refused to perform the test, he made an aggressive movement toward me and I withdrew my baton to protect myself. He grabbed the baton and attempted to wrench it out of my hand."

The robot had woken up and was finally starting to pour on the emotion.

"He grabbed my baton. I had to protect myself and my partner. I got the baton back from him and stuck him once on the knee and he went down. However, once he had fallen, before I could get a chance to secure the defendant, he grabbed me and wrestled me to the ground. Officer Shermer offered to help, but I waved him off and told him I had it and that he should attend to the other two suspects.

"I tried to handcuff him, but he was too strong, he wouldn't stay down. Then he grabbed my left arm, so only my right arm was free. I groped around my utility belt reaching for my Taser on the left, but I couldn't get it. All I could reach was my sidearm. As I drew it, he immediately grabbed it. I tried to get it back from him, but it was too late."

Albright choked with emotion and wiped the corners of his eyes.

"Can you continue?"

Albright held up his hand.

"Yes, yes. I tried to get my gun back, but he had already fired the first shot."

William nudged Brent and whispered, "He's lying!" Brent tapped his arm to keep him quiet, and whispered, "We'll have our chance," as Albright continued.

"After the first shot, the defendant tried to fire again, but I pushed the gun out of the way and, in the struggle, it went into the bushes."

"What did you do next?"

"I had to act quickly, so I used my baton to control the defendant. I needed to get him cuffed so I could help my partner. Once I had him down so he no longer posed a threat to my safety, I cuffed him and went to check on Officer Shermer and the other two suspects. He was down, laying on the ground. There was blood. I called for backup."

Officer Albright's voice started to crack. His amber eyes pooled.

"The two suspects appeared to be secure and cuffed, so I told them not to move and checked my partner's vital signs..."

Tears streamed down Albright's cheeks.

"I could not find....a pulse. He had lost a lot of blood and wasn't...breathing..."

Suddenly, Albright put his face in his hands and wept.

"I'm sorry. It's very difficult for me," he said, looking up at the jury in tears and wiping his eyes.

"Was your partner dead, Officer Albright?"

He nodded.

"You must give a verbal response, Officer Albright," said the judge.

Albright heaved a sigh.

"Yes, he was dead. I attempted first aid to revive him, but it was no use."

Not one single person in the jury box blinked during Albright's testimony, and Taylor paused to let it sink in. The seven women on the jury, whom Brent thought were his only hope, were fighting back tears and reaching into their purses for Kleenex. The five men were all nervously fidgeting in their seats. Brent glanced at Sarah, who had also registered the impact of Albright's testimony with a look of shock, and Albright shot his gaze directly at William, who appeared to be bathed in guilt.

"May we have a moment, Your Honor?" asked Taylor.

"Certainly. We'll take a five minute recess."

And the Oscar goes to....

Albright stepped down and exited the courtroom, a wounded man who had lost his comrade-in-arms.

After the full impact of Albright's testimony had had the opportunity to ferment and Albright resumed his role, Taylor had him demonstrate the location of the various items on his utility belt, photographs of which were admitted into evidence, and emphasized the point that Albright was right-handed. The Taser and pepper spray were on the left side of the belt, the gun and baton on the right, and two handcuff cases in the middle of the belt; which would have been behind Albright's back.

He reviewed Albright's shooting record, which was spotless, as well as his marksmanship, which was expert level. The emphasis, of course, was on the fact that Albright knew how to handle a firearm and it was highly unlikely that he could have botched it, leading to the shooting of his partner or the subsequent misfire.

Taylor's second act had taken up the whole court day, meaning that the jurors would take home and sleep on Albright's version of the story over the entire weekend before Brent had the opportunity to point out even one inconsistency.

CHAPTER THIRTY FOUR

Melinda had succeeded in getting a late afternoon appointment for Brent with Commander Owen of IAG, who often stayed at work after hours. By the time Brent got to his office, it was already seven o'clock, and Owen was closing up.

"Commander Owen?"

"You Marks? I was just stepping out for a bite to eat. Care to join me?"

Brent followed Owen, who directed them to a small, greasy spoon Mexican diner. The host, a short man with a handlebar moustache, greeted them at the door. They entered to the smell of fajitas and tacos and meat and beans.

"Buenos tardes, Commander Owen."

"Buenos tardes, Juan." Then, turning to Brent, "You like Mexican?"

"Yes," Brent said.

He took the question to be as a courtesy, as it appeared to him that Owen was a creature of habit and probably ate here every night (or at least every Friday night). Owen invited Brent to sit down at what must have been his "regular booth." The kitchen bustled with the sounds of the cooks slapping their utensils on steamy, sizzling grills and pans in rhythm with the bar and its whirling blenders.

"They've got the best guacamole in town here," said Owen, as the waiter greeted them with a generous bowl of it, as well as the traditional corn chips and salsa. A glance around the dining room at all the brown faces confirmed Owen's testimony. "You're of Mexican descent, aren't you?" he asked Brent.

"Close – Spanish. In fact, my father changed our last name to Marks from Marquez."

"No kidding. I'll have the usual, Javier. Marks?"

"I'll have the chicken fajitas with flour tortillas and a Corona, please."

"How's Jack holding up?" Owen asked, reaching for a chip and using it as a spoon to scoop up a hefty blob of avocado.

"He came out of his coma yesterday. That's the reason I called for this meeting."

"I'm glad he's out of the woods. Now, I told him – and I'll tell you – that I'm not about to help you guys defend a cop killer; but if Jack's found some kind of evidence to back up his hunch…"

"He has."

Brent outlined Jack's reports and the final revelation of his that Metro Unit 15-Robert-7 was involved in a prostitution ring in the San Fernando Valley.

"That's a very serious accusation," said Owen, between bites of his beef taco.

"I've tried to run down the hookers to see what they know, but so far, only one of them is talking."

"I suppose she won't do much for your case, anyway; her being a prostitute?"

"No, but it's all we've got, if I can get her into court."

"When will you need her?"

"Probably by Wednesday or Thursday. If I can even get her to come."

"Let me talk to her first. See if she would be willing to come in as a CI." The thought of a squadron of elite cops running a prostitution ring had Owen both disturbed and titillated.

* * *

"Brent, don't tell me you're going to spend Friday night with your prostitutes instead of me," pleaded Angela over the phone. She sounded a little perturbed.

"Angie, you know I have to keep in shape for you."

"All kidding aside, Brent, I miss you. When are you coming home?"

"I'll be home tonight, I promise. I just have to pass on Commander Owen's offer to…"

"The hookers."

"Well, yeah, one of them."

There was an uncomfortable silence on the phone for a moment. Then, "Give me a call when you're headed home. No matter how late. I'll be worried."

Brent was touched by Angela's concern. Not that he needed an FBI agent looking out for him, but it warmed him just knowing how much she cared.

Brent pulled up alongside the Sepulveda Boulevard hooker motels and waited. After a couple of hours, he had been propositioned by several ladies of the night in various shades of negligees and got rid of them by telling them he was waiting for "someone special." Knowing how much they cherished their own regulars, they had all smiled and went off to farm the rest of the area. Brent shivered as he thought how cold they must be. *I suppose that's the price you pay for advertising your goods.*

After a while, Brent pulled out his doggy bag from the Mexican restaurant and munched on some cold taquillos which he dipped in leftover guacamole that was beginning to turn brown, but still retained its fantastic taste. After the munchies were satisfied, he began to look around for a place to get some coffee to stay awake and help take the chill off, when he noticed Daisy getting out of a late model Chevrolet sedan.

She was heading in a direct line for one of the motel rooms when he called her over.

"Hey, honey, can you give me a minute to powder my... oh," she said, as she leaned into the window. "I thought we'd covered everything. I don't want any trouble."

Brent urged her to come in, and she reluctantly slipped into the car on a cloud of steamy perfume. Brent wasted no time in giving her Commander Owen's proposition.

"Oh no, no, no! I'm not going up against no cops," was her initial reaction, until Brent told her that she would be a confidential informant and that nobody would know her identity. He left out the part that she would be served with a subpoena and brought in on a bench warrant unless she came to court to testify.

Finally, after having delivered the message and not knowing whether she would see Owen or not, Brent said good-bye to Daisy and called "home" before he hit the freeway for Santa Barbara. It was 3 a.m.

CHAPTER THIRTY FIVE

The drive home was free of traffic and the crisp, moist blast of air from the window and its salty ocean smell kept Brent alert as he made his way up the coast. The moon blazed in the night sky, rippling off the water, as he entered the sleepy Harbor Hills community, with the expanse of the Santa Barbara Harbor looming beyond.

Brent carefully and quietly opened the front door, crept inside, and went downstairs to shower in one of the guest bedrooms, so as not to wake Angela. At 5 a.m. he finally slipped between the sheets and melted into the feather-soft mattress. Angela stirred and put her head on his shoulder as she slowly slid her calf over his leg. Brent was overwhelmed and overjoyed with comfort as he drifted into sleep.

* * *

As stressful as the trial was, William wished he was in the courtroom today. Anywhere would be better, actually. As he was called to breakfast, the putrid, stale air made him want to gag, much less want to eat. He had enjoyed the daily breaks from the smell, but then it was also harder to get used to when he was sent back to the jail. As he sat down at the cafeteria table, the taunting began again.

"Yo, how yo' coat goin' fo' offin' dat pig?" asked one bad-mouthed, buck-toothed troublemaker seated across from him. William simply ignored him.

"I'm talkin' to you!" said the black mountain, banging his hand on the table and leaning over into William with his lower lip sticking out. "Doncha got no manners?"

Sliding his tray onto the table, Curly sat down on the left side of the offending hulk, with his two lieutenants on the right.

"Put your lip back in your mouth, Ajax. That ain't no way to behave."

Ajax looked back in surprise, like he had been hit between the eyes with a stick. He backed off.

"Gotta protect my lawyer," said Curly, smiling. "How's my case goin, anyway?"

"We should probably talk about it privately, but it looks like I may have found something to help you. Of course, I could do more if I was out of here."

"If you get out of here, you won't forget about ol' Curly, will ya?"

"No, don't worry. I gave you my word."

After breakfast, William made his way back to the law library. He had been spending a lot more time there, and had been appointed as assistant librarian, which gave him more of an opportunity to work instead of wasting away in his cell. He split his time between research on his own case and Curly's, politely declining any new cases. The requests for new clients were frequent, but William had no time. Plus, the pay was not so good.

* * *

The smell of omelets smothered in cheese and the scent of freshly brewed coffee gently coaxed Brent awake as he lay in bed. *Nothing beats late, lazy Saturday mornings,* he thought. *Except maybe late, lazy Sunday mornings.* Saturday was often a day to work, but Brent found out right

237

away that, whatever work he had to do, he would have to sneak around to get to it with Angela there.

He shuffled into the living room, patting down his unruly hair, and into the kitchen where Angela was cooking and Calico was observing, swishing her tail back and forth impatiently.

"Morning," he said to them. The cat glanced at him quickly, then back at the cook.

"More like afternoon," said Angela.

"What time is it?"

"12:30."

Brent shook his head, grabbed a bottle of water, and collapsed into a kitchen chair. At least for now, he would get a little break from the trial.

Toward the end of the day, Brent was able to creep into his home office and turned on his computer, only to regret it, as his email box had overflowed with hundreds of unanswered messages for the week. He began the chore of trashing the irrelevant ones.

"Thomas, you've got a lawyer visit."   The Guard slid open the barred door.

William wondered what Brent could possibly want to discuss on a Saturday. To his surprise, it was Dr. Reading who greeted him with a smile.

"Dr. Reading, what are you doing here on a Saturday?"

"We have to continue your therapy, William. Wasn't it you who said we shouldn't waste the time we have?"

"Well, yes, but…"

* * *

Angela stayed over Saturday night, and, the following morning, she made it very clear that the day would be for relaxation only. But there was a catch. She proposed golf at the Sandpiper Golf Club.

The Sandpiper course was like Santa Barbara's version of Pebble Beach. Buttressed on a plateau right up against the beach, the fairways looked as if they lead right into the ocean. Although it was cold, the sun was shining and the air fresh.

Brent was glad that they were not keeping score when Angela's drive on the first tee was about 250 yards. She flashed a devilish smile at Brent as he sliced his first drive out of bounds.

"You didn't tell me you played on a semi-professional level," he said, after he thwacked the ball with his driver the second time.

"Just a few tournaments, with the guys."

By the ninth hole, it was obvious that Angela had beaten Brent's score, but he didn't care.

"Don't bother adding it up," he said, as he popped open a bottle of water and watched her going over the score card.

"Don't you want to know who's winning?" she asked, smiling.

"I think I know who's winning."

As they walked the course, Brent finally felt free. Being in nature and breathing the fresh air was exhilarating, and playing with Angela made it even better. It was just the rejuvenation Brent needed before going back into battle.

CHAPTER THIRTY SIX

Officer Albright resumed his place as a witness first thing Monday morning. He looked ahead at the jury with wide-open eyes of a rich amber, with hues of true blue and comforting forest green that professed that he could be trusted.

"Mr. Marks, you may proceed."

"Thank you, Your Honor. Officer Albright, when you stopped behind Mr. Thomas' car that night, you originally thought he had been drinking, is that correct?"

"Yes."

"But you never saw him driving that car, did you?"

"No, but it was obvious that he had been driving. The car was still running and he was in the driver's seat."

"But you never saw him driving the car, did you?"

"No."

"And you examined Mr. Thomas' eyes with your flashlight, correct?"

"Yes, I did."

"They didn't appear to be watery, did they?"

"No."

"And they didn't appear to be bloodshot either, did they?"

"I couldn't tell."

"Aren't watery eyes a symptom of alcohol consumption?"

"Yes, but not the only one. I needed to perform field tests to determine if he was under the influence of alcohol."

"Isn't one of the factors you consider in the decision to perform field tests whether the suspect exhibits any symptoms of alcohol use?"

Brent thought he could trigger a response from the police training that had been washed into Albright's brain.

"Yes."

"Besides watery and bloodshot eyes, isn't the smell of an alcoholic beverage on the breath also a symptom of alcohol use?"

"Yes."

"And you didn't smell an alcoholic beverage on Mr. Thomas' breath, did you?"

"There was a smell of alcohol in the car."

"Move to strike as non-responsive."

"Granted."

"You were close enough to Mr. Thomas to smell his breath, weren't you?"

"Yes."

"But you didn't notice a smell of alcohol on his breath, did you?"

"No."

"The smell of alcohol was from the other two occupants of the car, who were drunk, wasn't it?"

"Objection: calls for speculation."

"Overruled. Answer the question."

"I couldn't tell."

"Mr. Thomas complied when you asked him to perform the finger to nose test, didn't he?"

"He resisted."

"His only resistance was to tell you he wasn't under the influence of alcohol."

"That was how it manifested itself at that point, yes."

"But he performed the test, correct?"

"Yes, but then he failed to perform the walk and turn test."

Brent paused; then he went for Albright's buttons.

"Was that before or after you called him a nigger?"

"I never called him that."

"Was it before or after you shoved him with your baton?"

"I did no such thing."

"Didn't you push apart Mr. Thomas' legs with your baton during his performance of the finger to nose test?"

"I did not."

"You had your baton in your hand, didn't you?"

"Yes, I had it out to protect myself. The suspect was becoming belligerent and refused to follow instructions. I felt his behavior was escalating to possible violence."

"During the walk and turn test, you pushed him with your baton, didn't you?"

"No."

"Your baton made contact with Mr. Thomas' body, didn't it?"

"No."

Brent kept pushing. If Albright didn't crack, at least he would give a preview of William's testimony if he regained his memory.

"Mr. Thomas pushed your baton away from him, didn't he?"

"No, he grabbed it."

"He pushed it away because you shoved it into his back."

"I did not."

"Mr. Thomas questioned your treatment of him, didn't he?"

"No, he refused to follow instructions. He put my life in danger."

"Move to strike after 'instructions' Your Honor."

"Granted. The jury will disregard everything after 'instructions.'"

"You didn't like his resistance, did you Officer Albright?"

"I believed he compromised my safety."

"You didn't like his resistance, so you broke his knee."

"It was for my safety."

"He didn't attack you, but you broke his knee; isn't that what happened, Officer Albright?"

"No."

"And then you beat him with your baton."

"He refused to submit to arrest. He was threatening my safety."

"Move to strike as non-responsive."

"Granted. Answer the question."

"I struck him, yes. He was violent and resisting arrest."

"But you didn't suffer any injuries, did you?"

"He was violent!"

"Move to strike – non-responsive, Your Honor."

"Granted."

"You didn't have any injuries, did you, Officer Albright?"

"I was bruised up."

"Do you have any photos of your bruises?"

"No."

"Did you go to the hospital?"

"I was in emergency, you know, to get checked out."

"Did you have any broken bones?"

"No."

"Concussion?"

"No."

"Were you bleeding?"

"No, but…"

"Move to strike after 'but,' Your Honor."

"Granted."

"Officer Albright, you also kicked Mr. Thomas, isn't that correct?"

"He was attempting to wrestle me to the ground. I kicked him away to protect myself."

"You kicked him in his testicles, didn't you?"

"No. Certainly not on purpose. I kicked him away to protect myself."

"After you kicked him, he vomited, didn't he?"

"Yes."

"Then, after you broke his knee, broke his ribs, and kicked him in the stomach and testicles, you jumped on top of him."

"That's not how it happened!"

Brent read Albright's testimony from the preliminary hearing into the record, including the part where he claimed to have no independent recollection of attempting to handcuff William, other than what was stated in the police report.

"That was your testimony at the preliminary hearing, wasn't it?"

"Yes."

"After you broke Mr. Thomas's knee, you jumped on top of him, pulled out your gun, and stuck it in his face, didn't you?"

"Objection: compound."

"Overruled."

"I didn't!"

"And, as you pointed the gun in his face, you said, 'Nigger, your momma's not going to recognize you at your funeral', didn't you?"

"No!"

"No further questions, Your Honor."

After redirect, Benjamin Taylor put on Dr. Harvey Saperstein, the medical examiner who performed the autopsy on Shermer.

"Dr. Saperstein, would you please describe the cause of death of Officer Shermer?"

"Officer Shermer suffered a single gunshot to the abdomen which penetrated the stomach and liver, shearing tissue and causing hypovolemic shock to the rest of his organs."

"In layman's terms please, doctor."

"Certainly. The bullet entered the abdomen and passed through the stomach, and liver before exiting between the fourth and fifth back ribs.

Death occurred from the loss of blood supply to other vital organs." Dr. Saperstein's detailed autopsy report was admitted into evidence. On cross-examination, the doctor identified the location of the entry wound, the trajectory of the bullet, and the exact location of the exit wound.

Next, Taylor called an accident reconstruction expert who had charted the reported positions of William, Albright and Shermer, as well as Shermer's wounds, and who testified that, in his opinion, the fatal shot was fired from William's perspective. During his testimony, he showed charts and diagrams with graphed angles and vectors, showing the trajectory of the bullet. Brent examined the faces of the jury members. Most of them looked puzzled. Some, such as the two automobile workers, looked confused, and the accountant, whom Brent would have thought could appreciate all the technical stuff, was dozing off.

Brent had to tread very lightly with cross-examination of this witness. The best time to discredit his report would be when Brent's own expert was called to testify.

"Dr. Penson, your conclusions are all based on an original set of assumptions, isn't that correct?"

"Yes, they are."

"And those set of assumptions are data of where Officer Shermer was standing when he was shot and where William and Officer Albright were in relation to where he was standing, as well as the position of the gun, isn't that correct?"

"Among other things."

"All of these assumptions were gathered from the video, the autopsy report, and the police report of Detective Salerno; is that correct?"

"Yes."

"So, if one of these assumptions that you used was not correct, your conclusion could be flawed: isn't that correct?"

"I assure you, it's not."

"Move to strike as non-responsive."

"Granted."

"Doctor, if one of your assumed facts is not accurate, then your conclusion would also not be accurate: isn't that correct?"

"Yes, I suppose it is. But I'm sure they are all accurate."

"Were you there that night?"

"Objection: argumentative."

"Overruled."

"No, of course not."

By the time five o'clock rolled around, most of the jury looked like they were already working on their shopping lists and dinner recipes instead of listening to the trial.

CHAPTER THIRTY SEVEN

While it was true that Brent had no obligation to present a defense, the jury could go either way at this point. Brent had to push them over the boundaries of what was plausible into the realm of reasonable doubt. To accomplish this, he was equipped with two expert witnesses, two drunk eyewitnesses, and a client who couldn't remember anything. Not a great start, but one he had to accept and do the best with.

Brent checked with Commander Owen. Indeed, an investigation into possible corruption had been launched, and Daisy had agreed to be a confidential informant. Unfortunately, that was not going to help William's case. So, instead of sending a process server out to serve her, he opted for the personal touch.

"What the fuck is this?" Daisy fumed, pushing away the subpoena as if it were a rotten piece of meat as she flicked her cigarette into the street. "Your cop friend told me that everything I said was confidential."

"That's for his investigation. This is for my client's murder defense."

"And you wanna add another murder on top of that?" she asked, popping a piece of chewing gum in her mouth. "These guys don't care whether it's corruption or murder or what-not. They're gonna protect their own; which means I'm dead meat!"

"Hold on, hold on. I don't need you to testify about their prostitution ring."

"Oh no? What should I talk about? Donations for the Policeman's Ball? Blow jobs for the task force?"

"Daisy, look. I just need you to tell what you know about John Albright."

Her eyes opened fully and she stopped chomping on her gum.

"That nutty motherfucker? You must think I'm even crazier than he is."

"Just tell the jury what you told me."

"Yeah, right. And leave out the part about turnin' tricks 'n shit. I can't do it. Period. They'll kill me."

"You can testify on camera, secretly. I'll get a gag order and exclude your identity from everyone but the jury and the attorneys: they're barred from talking to reporters anyway, and they'll be sworn to secrecy."

She looked at Brent with distrust, as if he was a used car salesman pawning off his latest trade-in.

"The press won't know anything, which means the cops won't know anything. You're a confidential informant in an active police investigation. I'm sure the Court will grant the motion, and if it doesn't, I won't put you on."

"Really?"

"Really."

"I can trust you?"

"Scout's honor."

"You were a Scout? Jesus Christ!"

"Eagle."

"That means you believe in truth and justice, walking old ladies across the street, that kind of shit?"

"Pretty much."

"Well, Mr. Eagle Scout, you've got yourself a witness. Do you do wills?"

Brent smiled and handed the subpoena to Daisy.

After leaving Daisy, Brent prepared an affidavit for the motion and called Owen on his cell phone.

"Don't you believe in evenings?"

"Not during trials, I don't. I know you don't want to get involved, but I need to ask a favor. It's to protect your CI."

* * *

The final push to prepare was the only thing occupying Brent's mind when he checked into his hotel that night. Everything was ready –but not as ready as it could be. He shuffled papers, reviewed his outline, re-read reports.

As he tossed and turned in bed, Brent couldn't stop wondering if he had covered it all. Something had to be missing. Something always was. *But what is it?* He couldn't get it out of his head. Thinking was a mistake. Thinking of that phrase was an even worse one. The song 'I just can't get you outta my head' by Kylie Minogue took center stage as his main brain earworm.

After he finally fell asleep, it seemed like only seconds until the series of tiny dreams began, starring Brent as a freshman in college, missing his classes or showing up to them naked. He opened his eyes to find that the sweat from his neck had completely soaked his pillow. He looked at the clock. *Six a.m. Time to force myself to get up.*

CHAPTER THIRTY EIGHT

The first order of business was Brent's motion to present Daisy's in-camera testimony. The motion was heard in chambers, with only the judge, the court reporter and clerk, and the lawyers present. Usually the defendant would be the one to object to this secrecy because it impacted on his guarantee to confront witnesses against him; but it was William who was asking for it in this case. Law and order Judge Schwartz had no choice but to grant the motion, which was supported by a declaration from Commander Owen, and Benjamin Taylor was charged by the judge with keeping the identity of this witness secret from all prosecution witnesses. But it didn't go without a protest from him.

"This witness is not on the witness list, Your Honor."

"She's a rebuttal witness," said Brent.

"I'm sorry, Your Honor, but this is not fair. I understand your tentative is to grant the motion, but I think we need a proffer as to what this witness is going to say."

"Do you have an offer of proof, Mr. Marks?"

"Yes, Your Honor. Officer Albright has been described by witnesses as a model policeman who respects the law and has no propensity for violence. This witness will demonstrate a very different side to him: a side revealed in dealing with a detained prostitute where he acted with excessive force."

"Then it's inadmissible character evidence," piped Taylor. "I move to suppress it."

"That goes to the weight of the evidence, I'm afraid. Alleged prior acts of excessive force could be probative: we just have to determine whether they have a prejudicial effect," said Judge Schwartz.

Taylor shuffled out of chambers, a dog denied his bone, with his tail between his legs. Brent, on the other hand, had a tail like a saber. The playing field had finally become fair – at least as much as it could be.

260

"All rise. Department N of the Superior Court of the State of California for the County of Los Angeles is in session, the Honorable Adam Schwartz, Judge presiding," barked the Clerk.

"Good morning, ladies and gentlemen. Please be seated. Mr. Marks, are you ready to proceed?"

"Yes, Your Honor."

"Then you may call your first witness."

"I call Timothy Jones."

TJ faced the Clerk to be sworn in, then took a seat in the witness box. Brent, seeking to deflect Taylor's planned devastation of TJ on cross, led him to throw the jury some hints on what was to come. TJ introduced himself as a long-time friend of William's from childhood, with all the biases that came along with that. Brent had him describe their behavior at the baseball game, where he and Fenton had drunk a lot of beer and William had abstained, as he was the designated driver.

"Mr. Jones, you and Fenton Washington were drunk when you left the baseball game: is that correct?"

"Yes, we were. We had been drinking beer during the game, *like everybody else*. William was our designated driver, so he didn't have any beer."

Brent had TJ recount the traffic stop, his use of the Google Glass to record the videos, and the officers' behavior on the scene.

"Did you observe Officer Albright and William Thomas during the traffic stop?"

"I didn't take my eyes off them."

"About how far away from them were you during your observation?"

"About a car length. Fenton and I were handcuffed by the other policeman, and we were at the end of the car. Officer Albright and William were on the side of the road."

"On the passenger's side?"

"Yes, and so were we. I saw everything."

"Could you hear what they were saying as well?"

"Yes."

"Please tell the jury what you heard and saw from that point on."

TJ recalled Albright to be aggressive and impatient. He withdrew his baton "for no reason" and shoved William with it, and William pushed it away. Then, Albright became "crazy" and whacked his baton against William's knee, bringing him down, and then started hitting him all over with his baton, and kicking him. "Then he jumped on top of him."

"Was it at this point that you started the series of videos?"

"Yes. I just kept telling the Glass to record. I couldn't believe what I was seeing."

"What did you observe next?"

"The other policeman was telling Albright to take it easy; cool off."

"Those are the words he used?"

"No, it was something like, 'we've got him, now just cuff him.' Then Albright pulled his gun out and pointed it right at William's face."

"How far was the gun from his face?"

"Inches."

"Then what did you observe?"

"Albright said, 'Nigger, your momma's not gonna recognize you at your funeral!' and William pushed the gun away and it went off."

"In which direction did he push it?"

"To the left, I think. William's right handed."

"And you and Mr. Thomas and Officer Shermer were standing opposite William's feet, or his head?"

"His feet. I could see his feet, and the Officer's back was to us."

Brent had TJ identify all the raw video, which he would later connect up with the enhanced comprehensive tape with his video expert. Then TJ completed the story, which ended with Officer Shermer going down, and William losing consciousness. Then the video was played. From Brent's perspective, it couldn't be played enough.

It all seemed to go very well: that is, until Taylor began his annihilation on cross. Confidently, he rose and approached the witness box.

"Mr. Jones, do you remember the baseball game that night?"

TJ's mouth opened in confusion. He hesitated.

"Well, yes, of course."

"What was the score?"

"Final score?"

"Yes, the final score."

"3-2 Dodgers over the Cardinals."

"Do you remember the section of the parking lot you parked in?"

"No."

"How about the route you took home?"

"We took the 101."

"You remember taking the 101?"

"Yes."

"Where did you get on the 101?"

"I don't know."

"You don't remember?"

"No, I don't."

"What was the moon like that night?"

"I don't know. It was bright."

"Bright, like a full moon?"

"Yes, I think so."

"Would it surprise you that there was a new moon that night?"

"Yes. I could see fine."

"You know what a new moon is, don't you?"

"Yes, it's when the moon's a tiny sliver."

"Was the street well lit?"

"Yes, it was."

"Yet, parts of your videos were unintelligible because of lack of light, isn't that correct?"

"Yes, but…"

"Move to strike 'but,' Your Honor."

"Granted."

"You weren't aware that there was a burnt-out street lamp to the east, about 10 yards, were you?"

"No."

"Do you know what your blood alcohol level was that night?"

"The police told me, yes."

"You've been that drunk before, haven't you, Mr. Jones?"

"Yes, I have."

"And you've had occasion to wake up the next day after drinking and lose memory, haven't you?"

"What do you mean?"

"I mean, you've woken up with a hangover the day after drinking and realized that you had lost whole hours or minutes of time; isn't that correct?"

"Well yes, but not this time."

"Move to strike everything after 'yes,' Your Honor."

"Granted: the jury will disregard everything after 'yes.'"

"You were booked into the Twin Towers that night, weren't you, Mr. Jones?"

"Yes."

"And, before you were taken to jail, you gave Detective Salerno a statement: isn't that correct?"

"Yes, I did."

"Quoting from your statement, People's Exhibit number 12, *Question: 'How far were you away from the suspect and Officer Albright?' Answer: I'm not sure.'* Do you remember saying that?"

"No. I knew how far away we were."

"Move to strike after 'no,' Your Honor."

"Granted."

"Detective Salerno also interviewed you in the jail the next day, didn't he?"

"Yes, he did."

"Isn't it true that you asked him how long you had been there?"

"I don't remember asking him that."

"You lost a chunk of memory that night, didn't you, Mr. Jones?"

"Yes, but not until after the shooting."

Brent knew what the impact of cross-examination would be on TJ's testimony, so he resisted putting his hand to his forehead and looked straight ahead confidently, but that didn't stop the instant headache that had crept up on him during cross. William looked like a stranded shipwreck victim. The jury's faces were a collection of scowls. This testimony had not gone over well with them, especially the two teetotalers and the one recovering alcoholic, whom Brent would have kicked off the jury had he not run out of challenges. Impairment of memory is pretty common in cases of inebriation. The drinkers and recovering alcoholics on the jury knew it full well, as did the abstainers.

CHAPTER THIRTY NINE

Fenton's testimony was almost a carbon copy of TJ's, made even more of a train wreck by Taylor pointing out that Fenton and TJ had discussed what happened shortly after they had both been released from jail. Of course they had. It's human nature. Taylor made it look like a conspiracy; like they were getting their stories straight. It was his "cop's mind." He had spent so long working with the police, everything was a conspiracy to him. The truth never had any shades of grey – there was always a discernible line between black and white.

The courtroom was cleared of all spectators for Daisy McGovern's testimony.

"Ladies and gentlemen of the jury, the Court has granted a motion in this case to preserve and guard the identity of the next witness you are about to hear. We will be referring to her by the pseudonym, Miss D. This witness is a confidential informant in an ongoing police investigation, and you are not to discuss her, the fact that she has testified here, or her participation in the investigation with anyone. This admonition survives your jury service in court and you are bound by it after you are excused from duty."

Brent could see that this introduction lent Daisy a certain respectability with the jury, something which Taylor would not have to make much effort to tarnish. To ward off the obvious blow to her credibility that was coming, Brent elicited testimony from Daisy that would leave no doubt in the jurors' minds that she was, in fact, a prostitute, with a history of drug use as well as a criminal record. He could see already that the jury's opinion of her had shifted, but he had to lessen the explosive effect of these facts which would come out on cross-examination.

Daisy took the witness stand in her best, most conservative outfit: a mini dress that barely covered her butt cheeks and a halter top with no bra. The men on the jury took notice immediately, and the women on the jury looked as if they were on their way to join a chastity club.

Oh no, I forgot about the gum, Brent thought as Daisy chomped away like a sheep. *Well, maybe the judge won't notice.*

"Miss D, would you please dispose of your chewing gum," Judge Schwartz instructed nicely. "Gum chewing is not allowed in court."

"Gosh, I'm sorry, Judge," she said, and spit her gum into a Kleenex inside her "Hello Kitty" purse.

"Mr. Marks, you may inquire."

Brent stood up and approached the witness stand, keeping his eye on the jury box.

"Miss D, are you familiar with a person by the name of John Albright?"

"Yes, I am."

"I'm showing you a photograph. Can you identify the man in the picture?"

"Yes, that's John Albright. He's a cop."

"How did you first come to know Officer Albright?"

"My girlfriend and I were walking down the street one night and he pulled up to us in a police

271

car. He was on the passenger side and leaned out to talk to us."

"What's your girlfriend's name?"

"I'm not supposed to name her. It's in my statement to the police."

"Please continue," said the judge.

"Anyway, he asked us if we were working."

"Were you?"

"No. We were goin' for a burger."

"Then what happened?"

"He asked if we did 'freebies'. My friend said no."

"He said that any restaurant in town serves cops a free meal. They just walk in and sit down. He said it works the same way on the streets. She just said, "I said no."

"Then he got all mad and jumped out of the car. He grabbed my girlfriend and threw her against the car and said, 'assume the position.' Then he felt her up."

"What do you mean by, *felt her up*?"

"You know, he had his hands all over her boobs, pretending to search her, like she's gonna hide drugs and shit in her boobs, right?

"And then he stuck his creepy hand up her skirt. And he rubbed up against her butt with his pelvis, like he had the right to rape her or something."

"Move to strike, Your Honor. Speculation."

"Granted. The jury will disregard every word after *pelvis*."

"He said he never had any dark meat before, and asked her how much a nigger cost on Sepulveda Boulevard 'cuz where he came from, they were free."

"My friend cried and pulled away from him and he took his gun out and shoved it in her face."

"What did you do?"

"Nothin'. I just stood there. I told her to calm down, to do what he wanted, and then we could go. His partner told him to put the gun away and he did."

"Did he let you go?"

"Yeah, but he came around a lot after that."

"Move to strike everything after *yeah,* your Honor."

"Granted. The jury will disregard everything after *yeah.*"

Benjamin Taylor was frustrated, and it wore on his face. The Dudley Do-Right image of Albright had been tainted, but it was from an extremely unreliable source, and he had the ammunition to prove it.

"Ms. D, you've admitted to being a prostitute, correct?"

Daisy regarded Taylor with a boatload of attitude.

"I gotta make money. I wasn't born into no rich family."

"I see. And you've made money with other forms of criminal activity before, haven't you?"

"I've been arrested for shoplifting. I'm not proud of it."

"In fact, you were convicted of felony shoplifting just last year, isn't that correct?"

"Yes."

"And felony possession of cocaine two years ago, isn't that also true?"

"Yes."

"And you've spent some time in jail on these charges, haven't you?"

"I'm on probation now."

"I'm showing you an exhibit which purports to be a probation violation charge. Your name has been redacted, but can you identify it please?"

"Looks like a probation report."

"The charge was for lying to your Probation Officer, wasn't it?"

"Yes."

"You realize that you are under oath, Miss D, don't you?"

"Yes, of course."

"And that the penalties for perjury apply for not telling the truth here today?"

"Yes."

"Part of the terms of which are: you are not to break any laws, isn't that also true?"

"Yes."

"And perjury is against the law, isn't it?" Taylor spit. Daisy was losing control. Brent could see the anger building. Taylor was pushing her buttons.

"Yes! What do you expect me to do?" She raised her voice, moving her hands defensively.

"I expect you to tell the truth. Do you even know what that is?" he spurted back.

"Objection! Argumentative!"

"Sustained. Don't answer that."

"In fact, Miss D, you've never held down any kind of job other than stealing and prostitution, which are both illegal, isn't that correct?"

"Yeah, yeah, I'm a piece of shit!" Daisy screamed, standing up in her chair, arms flailing. "Is that what you want me to say? Yeah, I'm a low life, dirty whore, but that doesn't give some asshole cop the right to feel me up and then stick a gun in my face if he doesn't like the fact that I won't do what he wants because niggers should be for free!"

"Sit down, Miss D.!" warned the judge.

From fury to shame and misery, she sank down into the chair, bowed her head and cried into her hands.

Taylor objected like crazy, waving his arms like a child having a temper tantrum, and the judge struck the testimony, but it had woken up the slumbering jury better than a dose of electric shock therapy. That statement, the one they were instructed to forget, would be the only thing they would remember from Daisy McGovern's testimony.

CHAPTER FORTY

After the previous day's drama, Brent took advantage of the jury's newfound attentiveness to put on his video expert, along with the enhanced video. The jury watched the video with new eyes, as it was approximately twice the length of the original. But, alas, the "N" word did not appear anywhere, not even in the reconstructed audio track.

After the audio-visual presentation, Brent put on his ballistics and accident reconstruction expert, who expressed an entirely contrary opinion than the prosecution's expert had given. He also had charts and graphs of vectors and angles and, consistent with TJ's testimony, opined that if William had pushed the gun out of Albright's face with his right hand, he couldn't have caused the fatal shot. That could have only been done with a sweeping motion to the right. On cross examination, Taylor laid all the weaknesses of the testimony to bear.

"One of your assumptions on which you base your opinion is that the defendant pushed the gun to the left with his right hand, is that correct?"

"Yes."

"And the shot came from a right sweeping motion, correct?"

"Yes."

"So, for your opinion to be correct, the defendant would have had to push the gun to the left, is that right?"

"Yes."

"Let me pose to you a hypothetical question, Mr. Samuelson. Assume all the facts in your set of assumptions except for one: that fact being that the defendant pushed the gun to the right instead of left. This change of assumption would change your opinion as well, wouldn't it?"

"It may."

"And if the defendant had pushed it to the right, he could be the shooter; isn't that true?"

"It is possible."

"Assuming all facts in your assumption except for one: that if he didn't push the gun at all, but took it out of Officer Albright's hands, he could be the shooter, isn't that right?"

"It is also possible."

Brent rehabilitated Samuelson as much as he could, but he hadn't changed his original assessment that none of the expert's opinions would have an overwhelming effect on the jury. Unfortunately, it would all come down to their collective gut feeling on whether to believe Albright's story. He needed something more for them to go against Albright. He needed William. At the lunch break, he turned to William and asked, "Are you ready?"

"For what?"

"To testify."

"I thought you said I wasn't going on the stand unless I remember."

"Then I suggest you remember all that you can. I think it's what we need to get this case out of the mud."

* * *

"I call William Thomas."

William limped to the witness stand. His hands were shaking and he hoped the jury would not notice. This was the first time he had ever been in court as a witness. All of his time had been spent on the other side of the counsel table. The Clerk swore William in.

"Do you solemnly swear or affirm to tell the truth, the whole truth, and nothing but the truth so help you God?"

"I do."

William took his place in the witness chair and, in response to Brent's questioning, told the jury about his life, his career, and, finally, he reached the point where Albright and Shermer had stopped his car.

"The officer asked me if I had been drinking."

"No, no. I'm the designated driver. Look officer, I'm not under the influence of alcohol."

"Did I ask you for your opinion, nigger?"

"Excuse me? Did you say 'nigger'?"

"I didn't say anything. You said it. And isn't that what you people call each other?"

William knew he should keep quiet, but the anger started to boil inside.

"Well, if we people did, that doesn't give you the right to say it," he retorted.

"You ain't got any rights here, boy, 'cept the right to remain silent, and I suggest you use it."

"Why? Am I under arrest?" asked William, ignoring the cop's warning.

"Stand with your legs together, head back, arms out straight. Close your eyes."

"I kept telling him I wasn't drunk, and he kept telling me to shut up. I knew I probably should have just stayed quiet, but he had no right treating me like I was worthless, like I was not even a human being."

"I told you I'm not drunk."

Albright glared at William. He had taken just about enough lip.

"Be quiet. Now do the same with the right index finger."

William extended his arm, and touched his right index finger to the tip of his nose. The cop withdrew his baton and forced William's legs apart with it.

"I was doing what he told me, but he just kept pushing me with his baton. He was out of control."

"Hey, don't hit me with that. I'll do whatever you say."

"Shut up. Now I want you to walk a straight line, heel to toe, until I tell you to stop."

He shoved William forcefully with the baton in his spine. William winced with pain, and shoved the stick away with his hand.

"You don't need to keep hitting me with that stick. I'm doing everything you..."

"Why did you push the officer's baton away, William?"

"It was a reaction, I guess. The first time he hit me with it, he forced my legs apart with the club before I even got the chance to do it myself. He was taunting me, you know? Like he wanted me to resist."

"Move to strike as speculation," barked Taylor.

"Granted. The jury will disregard everything after *myself.*"

"The question is still pending," said Brent.

"So when he shoved me with it, it hurt, and I pushed it away. He didn't have any right to hurt me."

"What happened then?" asked Brent.

"I'm not…I can't. The memories are hard to deal with. I…"

"You have to tell the jury what happened! Do it now!" Brent said, raising his voice.

"Objection! Harassing the witness."

"It's his witness. Overruled."

"What happened, William?"

William sighed, heaved back his shoulders, and said, "It was scary. He attacked me with that stick, whacked me in the knee, and I went down."

"Then what happened?"

Right Brent, then what happened? What the hell happened?

"William? Tell us!"

William recoiled in shock as a black curtain seemed to open before his eyes.

And the systems just come back, one by one.

His eyes widened and he took a deep breath to face his demons.

Albright pummeled William with his baton, a wild animal out of control, as TJ and Fenton looked on in terror. The blows kept coming and coming. Then, he kicked and kicked, then beat him with the stick, over and over again. William tucked his head under his shoulder to try to protect it from the blows, but the baton connected and the lights went out, back on, out, then on again. William couldn't control his arms and legs. He felt the blast of each impact, his heart was pounding out of control, and his vision narrowed.

Albright kicked William in the ribs, again and again, and William felt the air knocked out of him. He couldn't breathe. He tried to crawl away, but Albright kicked him in the balls. The pain seared his soul as he moved his hands to cover and protect himself. Another strong kick in the stomach, and William felt like his guts were coming out of his throat. His dinner was, and he threw it up all over the pavement.

"You barfed on my shoe, nigger!"

"John," said the second cop. Albright ignored him, jumped on top of William. That made the second cop recoil in surprise, and he stood back. William drifted in and out. It was if all of the blood had drained away from his brain.

"John, we've got him for resisting arrest. Just cuff him."

"Fuck that, Davey," the rogue cop said in a surprisingly calm-sounding voice. "This shit stain put the lives of two police officers in danger *and we had no choice". William felt himself going in and out of consciousness, like he was between dreaming and waking up.*

"Officer Shermer was telling him to stop, just to handcuff me, but he wouldn't listen. He was like a wild animal."

Slipping in and out now, William thought to crawl away, but Albright had jumped on top of him and it was impossible to escape. He opened his eyes and was face to face with the barrel of a gun.

"I knew he was going to kill me then. I thought about my pretty Sarah and my kids, Danny and Sissy, and how I'd never get to see them again. And all because I was stupid enough to try to keep a cop from shoving me around with his stick. Now I was going to die. I should have just let him push me around. I wasn't drunk."

"What happened next, William; what happened?"

Tears streaked down William's cheeks as he recalled the memory for the very first time. "He pushed that gun against my forehead. Then, he said, 'Your momma's not gonna recognize you at your own funeral.' He was not just going to kill me, he was going to *erase* me. So my mom wouldn't even recognize me. I got up all my strength and shoved his gun away as hard as I could."

"In which direction?"

"To the left. I pushed as hard as I could with my right hand, but I felt him pushing it back toward my face. And then it went off."

"Was your finger on the trigger?"

"No! His was!"

A hush fell over the courtroom like a descending fog, eclipsing all senses.

Brent stared ahead, partially from disbelief and partially from exhaustion. All eyes of the jury were on William, who was looking at Sarah with eyes that beckoned her to take him home.

Judge Schwartz broke the silence.

"Do you have any further questions, Mr. Marks?"

"No, Your Honor."

"It is now 4:50 p.m. Court will adjourn until tomorrow morning at 9 o'clock."

CHAPTER FORTY ONE

After court, Brent went directly to Valley Presbyterian, where he found Jack sitting up in the bed playing with his iPhone. The color was back in Jack's skin. The bruises had turned a yellowish green and were fading. He looked alive again.

"Hey, Jack."

Jack looked at Brent anxiously. He threw the phone down on the bed.

"Brent, you have to get me out of here. There's nothing to do and the food is terrible."

"That ought to convince them to release you."

"Really: if I stay here one more day, I'm going to go nuts. Bring me up to date on the Thomas case."

"William had a breakthrough today."

"He remembered?"

"Everything. Right on the witness stand. And right after Daisy Mc Govern ripped Taylor a new one during his cross-examination. It was like a chapter out of Perry Mason."

"No!"

"Yes. I finally think it's turned around. But, you never know with juries. I'd take a judge every time, unless of course I'm guilty."

"You'll kill it in final argument," Jack said, confidently.

"Brent?"

"Yeah?"

"I'm sorry I couldn't finish the investigation."

"You did, Jack. We got what we needed: we got Daisy."

* * *

Brent expected cross-examination to take about half a day, maybe longer. Then he would rest his case and, if Taylor had no rebuttal, they would move on to final argument. This was perhaps the most important part of a trial. The jury would be cautioned not to regard it as evidence, but all they had heard up to this point were two exactly opposite versions of the same story and a bunch of technical stuff.

The judge would read them a collection of instructions summarizing the law to apply to whatever disjointed facts they were able to remember. The instructions had been written in layman's legalese by a gaggle of lawyers and judges and they would be as familiar to the jury as the geography of Mars. Someone had to make sense out of it and give them an easy solution to the puzzle, and that would be Taylor. Brent's function would be to point out everything that was confusing and didn't make sense and then, for the home run, lay out the only conclusion that they could logically follow.

Brent grabbed his gym bag and headed for 24 Hour Fitness, hoping that a good workout would clear his mind. His closing statement was outlined, but he had to nail it in the delivery. As

289

he jogged on the treadmill, he argued to himself, making his presentation as his body went through his routine.

CHAPTER FORTY TWO

William retook the witness stand, as prepared as he could be for the onslaught to come. Taylor perched at the side of counsel table, looked at William with distrust and suspicion, then looked back at the jury to make sure they had registered it.

"Mr. Thomas, you've spent several weeks in the County Hospital before this trial, haven't you?"

"Yes."

"Where you were under psychiatric care?"

"I was undergoing therapy."

"Memory therapy, isn't that correct?"

"Objection, Your Honor: privilege."

"Counsel, approach the bench."

Once at the bar with the court reporter, the judge said, "Your objection is premature, Mr. Marks. The psychotherapist-patient privilege applies to communications between the therapist and patient. I will take up your objection when and if the need arises. For now, it will be overruled."

Taylor brimmed with fortitude on his way back to the counsel table, then turned and faced William confidently.

"You were undergoing memory therapy, isn't that correct?"

"It was therapy for post-traumatic stress. Memory recovery was part of it."

"And the therapy was administered by Dr. Lucille Reading, correct?"

"Yes."

"And the reason you were undergoing memory therapy was that you couldn't remember anything that happened the night Officer Shermer was shot, isn't that correct?"

"I couldn't remember all of it."

Taking a further risky step, Taylor ventured into the unknown.

"You had hypnosis therapy, didn't you?"

"Among other things, yes."

"And you were administered hypnotic drugs, weren't you?"

"Yes."

"You couldn't remember anything about the gun, could you?"

"Before?"

"Yes, before your therapy."

"Just bits and pieces."

"Just bits and pieces," Taylor repeated, as he regarded the jurors. Then, he surged forward into the darkness. "In fact, originally, in those bits and pieces of your memory, Mr. Thomas, you thought you shot Officer Shermer, didn't you?"

"Not exactly."

"Not exactly. Most of us would know exactly if we *killed* someone or not…"

"Objection. Argumentative!"

"Sustained. The jury will disregard counsel's comment and make no inference from it."

Taylor looked at the jury, then at William.

"One of those bits and pieces of your memory was that you shot Officer Shermer, wasn't it?"

"That's not what happened."

"But, before your memory therapy, that's what you *thought* happened, wasn't it?"

"I thought it could have happened. But now I know that it didn't."

"That's very convenient, Mr. Thomas, but what I would like to ask is…"

"Objection! Argumentative!"

"Sustained. The jury will disregard the question."

"You thought it could have happened." Taylor regarded the jury with a look of affirmation. "And when you were lying on the ground that night, you grabbed Officer Albright's weapon, didn't you?"

"I pushed it."

"You weren't going to let him arrest you, were you Mr. Thomas?"

"He was trying to kill me!"

"Move to strike: non-responsive and speculative, Your Honor."

"Counsel approach."

"The defendant has asserted self-defense, Your Honor," said Brent. "And his state of mind is relevant to that claim of self-defense."

"Your Honor, it is clearly outside the scope of the question, which called only for a yes or no answer."

"The defendant's perception is relevant to self-defense. I'm going to let the answer stand."

Taylor moved back to counsel table, still standing and still resolute, and then he violated the principal law of cross-examination. He asked a question to which he did not know the answer. It was a gamble – black or red, point or craps – and Taylor knew it.

"When did you have your sudden recovery of memory, Mr. Thomas?"

"Yesterday," said William, humbly.

"Yesterday," repeated Taylor, looking at the jury with disbelief. "Yesterday, here in court, during your testimony?" he asked, as if it were a surprise.

"Yes."

"So, yesterday, here in court, while you were on the witness stand, your memory suddenly reappeared, is that correct?"

"Objection: argumentative!"

"It's cross-examination, Your Honor."

"Overruled."

"Answer the question, Mr. Thomas. Did your sudden reappearance of memory occur while you were on the witness stand?"

"Yes."

"And immediately before that, it was just bits and pieces, correct?"

"Yes."

"So, yesterday, when testifying on your own behalf, you suddenly remembered every detail of what happened that night that Officer Shermer was shot?"

"Objection: asked and answered!"

"Overruled."

"Yesterday," Taylor repeated, "when testifying on your own behalf, you suddenly remembered every detail of what happened that night that Officer Shermer was shot; isn't that correct?"

"Yes."

"I'm going to ask about some things you do remember."

"Objection: argumentative."

"Sustained.

"Withdraw the question, Your Honor. When Officer Albright first approached you in your car that night, didn't you tell him to turn off his flashlight?"

"No. I asked him if he had to shine it in my face."

"You initially refused to exit the vehicle, correct?"

"No, he asked me to step out of the car and I asked him 'what for?'"

"So you resisted stepping out of the vehicle, correct?"

"I got out of the vehicle. I just asked him why he was making me get out."

"And you resisted when he asked you to turn around and put your hands on the vehicle, isn't that correct?"

"No, I didn't resist. I protested, but I didn't resist."

"And you denied having an open container of alcohol in your car, isn't that correct?"

"I expressed surprise. I didn't know about it."

"Then, when the officer questioned you about whether you had been drinking, you became belligerent."

William remained steadfast, faced Taylor and then looked at the jury.

"He called me a nigger. I'm no nigger."

"Move to strike as non-responsive, Your Honor."

"Denied."

"You interfered with the field sobriety tests, didn't you?"

"I didn't."

"You kept repeating to Officer Albright that you were not drunk, is that correct?"

"Yes."

"And you denied having an open container of alcohol, didn't you?"

"I didn't know about it."

"You refused to perform the walk and turn test, didn't you?"

"No."

"During the test, you reached for Officer Albright's baton, didn't you?"

"He was shoving me with it."

"Move to strike as non-responsive."

"Granted: answer the question please."

"You reached for his baton, correct?"

"I pushed it away."

"So you touched his baton, correct?'

"Yes."

"And you pushed it back at him, correct?"

"Yes."

Taylor checked the jury to make sure they were paying attention. All eyes were on him. He moved closer to the witness stand in an accusatory fashion.

"And, after Officer Albright applied bodily force to pin you down, you grabbed his gun, didn't you?"

"I pushed it out of the way."

"You touched his gun, correct?"

"Yes. I had to!"

"And you tried to take it away from him?"

"I pushed it away."

"You wanted to shoot Officer Albright didn't you?"

"He was trying to kill me."

"Move to strike as non-responsive."

"Granted.   The jury will disregard the answer."

Taylor was face to face with William now, continuing the standoff, compelling the outcome.

"You intended to shoot him, didn't you?"

"He had the gun in my face! He was going to shoot me! If one of us was getting shot, it was going to be him!"

"No further questions." Taylor kept a lid on his happiness, but Brent could see him hiding behind a curtain of smug.

CHAPTER FORTY THREE

Dr. Reading was on Brent's witness list, but he hadn't intended to call her unless he absolutely had to. Taylor's casting doubt on William's memory on cross-examination had made it a necessity.

Brent elicited Dr. Reading's qualifications: her PhD in psychology from Berkeley, her Juris Doctor in law from Berkeley, her M.D. from UC San Francisco School of Medicine, her 25 plus years' experience as a board certified psychiatrist, and her numerous articles in medical journals about the subject of memory therapy. Taylor chose not to voir dire her, and accepted her qualifications. *He has to have something up his sleeve,* thought Brent. Dr.

Reading was dressed conservatively, like a doctor, but she had a look that drew men's attention. Her auburn hair had a shine to it, even under the fluorescent light. The men on the jury could not take their eyes off her. The women on the jury were asking themselves how she looked so good for her age, and who did her hair?

"Dr. Reading, during Mr. Thomas's incarceration, did you diagnose him with any type of medical condition?"

"I diagnosed him with post-traumatic stress disorder following the shooting of Officer Shermer."

"What symptoms led you to this diagnosis?"

"Depression, irritability, suppressed memories, nightmares. And I confirmed the diagnosis with a blood test."

"Can you describe this blood test?"

"It's a brand new test, still in its testing stages. It's based on a blood marker associated with PTSD that Doctors from Icahn School of Medicine discovered.

"The test is designed to identify the marker, and it was found to be present in William's blood."

"Did you prescribe a treatment program of therapy for Mr. Thomas?"

"I prescribed a plan to treat his PTSD and attendant declarative memory dysfunction."

"Could you explain declarative memory dysfunction?"

Dr. Reading faced the jury. Just her demeanor and appearance seemed to set them at ease. It was if they had all taken a place on the couch in her office. She described declarative memory dysfunction as a very common condition in cases of post-traumatic stress disorder. In PTSD, memories associated with the stress trigger, a horrendous trauma, often make the patient feel like he is experiencing the trauma all over again.

"The condition is very common in cases of rape, child abuse, combat, and with victims of violent crime. The brain, in order to protect itself, avoids recollection. Think of it like putting something away that gives you bad feelings to look at."

"Could you please describe the treatment plan?"

"Yes. The idea is to train the brain to recall the memories without triggering the trauma. It involved very simple behavioral therapies, such as prolonged exposure, which consisted of having William repeat all he could remember from the incident, over and over, in every detail he could recall. This helped to ease his anxiety and depression."

Dr. Reading outlined the therapies she used with William, including eye movement desensitization, exposure therapy, and hypnosis.

"Was any of this therapy effective?"

"Not when I was treating him, but I understand he did have a breakthrough and spontaneous recall."

"Is that unusual in cases of PTSD?"

"Not at all. Often patients recall their painful memories spontaneously as a result of encountering reminders outside of therapy."

"Knowing what you do about Mr. Thomas' recall in court, have you formed an opinion within a reasonable degree of medical certainty on the reason for his spontaneous recall?"

"Yes I have."

"Please tell the jury your opinion, doctor."

"It's my opinion that William experienced stressors during his incarceration that equaled or exceeded those which he experienced during that night, and, hearing the reminders of the event during the trial, and especially examination under oath, he had a full spontaneous recovery. I would rate the PTSD therapy as a success."

"Thank you, doctor."

Taylor looked as if he was holding back a surprise that would make him explode, as he went into his cross-examination.

"Dr. Reading, are you aware of the criticism of memory therapy and fabricated memories in the medical community?"

"Yes, I am aware that studies have been conducted that accuse memory therapists of planting or fabricating memories in cases of child abuse."

"Are these peer-reviewed studies?"

"As far as I know, yes."

"Dr. Reading, you were hired by the defense in this case, were you not?"

"I was not. Brent Marks referred me to Mr. Thomas, but it was he and he alone who hired me."

"To reconstruct his memories of the event?"

Dr. Reading's face reddened, and her brows furrowed at the implication that she had manufactured William's memories.

"Not at all! I was hired to diagnose and treat William for his PTSD. His recovered memory was a bi-product of that treatment, not the point of it."

"But your primary objective was to restore his memory of the event, is that correct?"

"No, it was not. My primary objective was to treat his disorder. The dysfunctional memory was a symptom of it and, if William could regain his memory, it would be part of his recovery. William regained his memory on his own."

"Or made it up," Taylor said, looking in the direction of the jury.

"Objection: argumentative!"

"Sustained. The jury will disregard Mr. Taylor's comments."

"Doctor, this blood test you used to confirm your diagnosis of PTSD: it's not accepted in the medical community, is it?"

"No, not yet. I said it was still in the process of being tested. But I made the diagnosis before doing the blood test."

"Do you often use methods not accepted in the medical community, doctor?"

"I resent the implication!" Dr. Reading was boiling. Her lips turned down at the corners and her eyebrows puckered. "I always keep in touch with the latest tests and methods of therapy. It doesn't mean that I use unreliable methods."

Brent took some time to re-examine Dr. Reading on redirect, mostly so the jury could re-establish those warm and cozy feelings that she had instilled in them from the beginning. And these were the emotions that Brent hoped the jurors would tuck themselves into bed with, as Court conveniently adjourned for the day at this point.

CHAPTER FORTY FOUR

The trial had overshot its two week estimate, but Brent was fairly confident that they would present their closing summations the next day, so he went home: the nicest place he could think of to rest and prepare for the argument of his life (and William's).

The evening was crisp but not too cold, and the traffic was light as Brent made his way up the 101 freeway. He dreamed of a vacation after the trial; but not some faraway place. No, the balcony of his Harbor Hills home was where he had set his sights. He avoided the office, where there could be nothing good waiting for him, and remembered his immigrant client from Yugoslavia, Dusan. Dusan had told him that the most important thing he learned about living in the States was to avoid the mailbox: you never found any good news in there. So he took old Dusan's advice and went straight to the house where, instead of finding bad news, he found a not-so-hungry cat and her caretaker.

"Brent, you're home!"

"Yeah, how about that!"

Angela beamed and threw her arms around Brent. It was the best welcome home he had ever received. Even the cat seemed happy to see him, as she slinked around their legs.

"Sit down and relax," said Angela as she led him by the hand to the couch, where he plopped down. She sat next to him and said, "Maybe we should go out and have a nice, relaxing dinner at your favorite place."

Brent smiled. "*This is* my favorite place. Why don't we just stay here?"

As Angela prepared dinner, Brent went through his trial notes and closing outline one last time. If he wasn't ready now, he never would be.

* * *

Detective Henry Dumont sat in his unmarked Dodge Challenger on Van Nuys Boulevard, laying low and observing every one of the comings and goings on the street as he patiently waited. Dumont was proud of his job, which he thought was the most important one at the LAPD. At first he didn't like his assignment to IAG. All his buddies had turned against him. He was no longer welcome anywhere.

It wasn't obvious; just a feeling that he got whenever someone said hello (or didn't). But during the past three years his eyes had been opened to the fact that not every person in service had done it for the same reasons, and the ones who had, had been tainted by what they had seen and what they had gone through. For Dumont it was very simple. There was no room for dishonesty on the police force.

He had been charting the comings and goings of 15-Robert-7 for the last several days and had noticed nothing unusual. But this night they had deviated from their pattern. This night they had been crawling around this neighborhood, taking in the neighborhood prostitutes, and Dumont had recorded it all on his night vision camcorder.

311

CHAPTER FORTY FIVE

"Do the People have any rebuttal?" asked the Judge.

"Yes, Your Honor."

"Please proceed, Mr. Taylor."

"The People call Dr. Lawrence Cartwright."

Dr. Cartwright was a scientist, psychiatrist, and an attorney. He had received his PhD in behavioral psychology from UC Berkeley, an MD from Stanford School of Medicine, and a JD from Harvard Law School. He had testified as an expert in hundreds of cases relating to memory therapy, and was the author of the leading articles on false memory implantation.

"Doctor Cartwright, you are an outspoken critic of repressed memory therapy; are you not?"

"Yes, I am."

"Can you explain to the jury why?"

"Of course." Cartwright spoke directly to the jury, ignoring Taylor. The jury members were his pupils, and he was there to educate them.

"The human memory is malleable and responds to suggestion. It's not like a file cabinet or hard disk on a computer, which files away every memory until it is recalled. Memories of events are almost always a combination of factual traces of sensory information mixed with emotions, with the blanks filled in by imagination. That is why you will hear so many different interpretations of the same event."

"How does the fabrication of memories occur, doctor?"

"Remember what I said about the brain's tendency to fill in the blanks with imagination? This is the reason why so-called "repressed memories" may not be memories at all, but fill-ins by the imagination during therapy; especially hypnotic therapy."

Dr. Cartwright explained to the jury the famous "Lost in the Mall" experiment of Elizabeth Loftus, the memory expert who was known for her research on the subject of memory fabrication. In the experiment, subjects were given summaries of real childhood events written by family members, along with a fictitious account of being lost in a shopping mall. All the subjects recalled the shopping mall incident with great detail.

"This is why the American Psychological Association states that, without corroboration, it is not possible to distinguish recovered memories from those that have been fabricated."

Taylor then posed a hypothetical question to the doctor in which he was asked to assume a man who had experienced great physical and emotional trauma and was unable to recall anything but bits and pieces of the event. The man underwent memory therapy for several weeks with no results, including hypnosis, eye movement desensitization and reprogramming, (called exposure therapy), then listened to witnesses' testimony of the event in court and then experienced spontaneous total recall.

"Doctor, based on this hypothetical, are you able to reach an opinion to a degree of medical certainty about whether the "memory recovery" was false?"

"Yes. Under these circumstances, total spontaneous memory recovery is highly unlikely and should be suspect, absent corroborative evidence."

"Thank you, doctor."

"Cross-examination?"

"Thank you, Your Honor. Doctor, are you saying that spontaneous memory recovery is impossible?"

"No."

"And would matching accounts by other eye-witnesses be considered corroborative evidence?"

"If they were reliable, they may."

Brent chose not to continue cross-examination because, at this point, the doctor was not going to "crack." He was more likely to repeat his testimony, which could then possibly find a permanent place in the psyches of the jurors.

There being no more rebuttal testimony, Judge Schwartz called a 15-minute recess.

"Counsel, be prepared for your closing statements when we return."

316

The judge cautioned the jurors that what the attorneys had to say was not evidence, and they should not consider it as such. Benjamin Taylor strode to the podium, rested his notes on the surface of it, put his hands on its sides, and took a long, hard look at the jury, like they were an athletic team and he was the coach. This would be his pep talk before the big game.

"Ladies and gentlemen, I told you at the beginning of this trial that this was a very simple case. Now you can see that what I said was true. What is complicated is not the case, but the fact that we cannot exist as a society without laws, and we cannot have laws without the means for their enforcement.

"This means that, just as you all sit in judgment here, we must rely on our peace officers to make split-second judgments in the field of law enforcement. Sometimes these split-second judgments are, literally, a matter of life and death.

"So that our police can enforce the law and protect us from violent crime, they are entitled to use more force to protect lives and property than we are, as normal individuals and members of our society."

317

Taylor advised the jury that the judge would instruct them that it was not their job to examine Officer Albright's conduct and the decisions he made through the glass of hindsight, to determine what he should or should not have done when he made the decisions that he made to ensure his safety and the safety of his partner. Every situation is different, and no two police officers facing the same potentially violent situation will react in exactly the same manner.

"Mr. Marks will tell you that, if you're stopped by a police officer, you need not blindly do everything he says with a big smile on your face. However, you are not allowed to use force to resist an arrest, whether it is lawful or not, and that's exactly what the defendant did."

Taylor looked at William over his shoulder, then back at the jury, and explained that William had been charged with murder in the second degree, with a special circumstance of murder of a police officer. The charge included a charge of manslaughter, in case second degree murder didn't stick.

"To prove murder beyond a reasonable doubt, the People must prove three things: One, that the defendant caused the death of Officer David Shermer; Two, that he either intended to kill or that the natural and probable consequences of his actions were dangerous to human life and that he knew that; and Three, that the killing was without lawful excuse or justification. Ladies and gentlemen, I will demonstrate to you that the People have proven each of these elements beyond a reasonable doubt."

Taylor went to the chalkboard and wrote, *The Defendant caused the death of Officer Shermer.*

"First, the People have proven beyond a reasonable doubt that the defendant caused the death of Officer Shermer. Officer Albright testified that he had a dangerous situation on his hands after he contacted the defendant. First, the defendant resisted Officer Albright's instructions. Next, when Officer Albright chose to display an appropriate degree of force so as to minimize the defendant's risk to his safety and to the safety of Officer Shermer, the defendant forcefully grabbed the baton of Officer Albright, forcing him to use it on the defendant.

"Officer Albright is a respected and decorated officer who has no history of discipline. The only testimony against his character was given by a convicted felon who is also a street prostitute. As the judge will instruct, you may consider that in deciding whether to believe her testimony or not.

"On the other hand, Officer Albright's testimony is corroborated by the physical evidence, as testified to by our expert witnesses. The defendant's fingerprints were on the gun. The People's expert testified that the gun had been tampered with. Even the defendant himself admits touching the officer's gun.

"Detective Salerno testified that, given the limited amount of choices of force Officer Albright had when the use of bodily force did not work, it was reasonable to pull his gun."

Taylor explained that the jury was not allowed to simply stack up the witnesses against each other and make a decision based on how many told the same story. They had to evaluate each witness's credibility and make a decision as to whether to believe them and what weight to give to their testimony, if any.

"The defendant tells a very different story: a story upon which we cannot lend any credence because, up until the very point of his testimony, he remembered nothing past the point of his reluctance to perform the field sobriety tests. You cannot lend any credibility to his so-called spontaneous memory, as the only corroboration of it is by his two witnesses, who were both drunk at the time and admitted to alcohol-related memory lapses."

Taylor went over every witnesses' testimony and all the physical evidence, methodically, making sure that the jury was with him. As he spoke of the physical evidence, he set each exhibit on the counsel table. Front and center on display was the murder weapon.

"So, as you see, the evidence very clearly points to only one inference, and that is that the defendant caused the death of Officer Shermer. And I will go one step further. You don't even have to believe that the defendant actually shot the gun to hold that he caused Officer Shermer's death. There is no question that the defendant tampered with Officer Albright's gun, and this leads us to the second element of murder."

Taylor returned to the chalkboard and wrote, *The People have proven beyond a reasonable doubt that the defendant intended to kill or that he knew that the natural and probable consequences of tampering with the gun were dangerous to human life.*

Taylor next explained the concept of transferred intent, which meant that if they found that William intended to kill Officer Albright, or acted in reckless disregard of the danger of his actions to human life, but by mistake or accident killed Officer Shermer, the crime was the same as if he had killed the intended person.

"You heard the defendant himself admit that one of them was going to die, and it wasn't going to be the defendant."

Taylor picked up the gun from the counsel table, then walked back to the lectern, brandishing it like a movie prop.

"As Mr. Marks pointed out during the trial, a gun is used to inflict great bodily injury or death. The People don't need to prove that the defendant had the intent to kill because, when he tampered with this gun, he knew that the natural and probable consequences of that act was dangerous to human life, and that was the equivalent of intent in the eyes of the law."

Using my words for your cause, thought Brent. Taylor was an extremely clever manipulator.

Taylor approached the board and wrote, *There was no justification or excuse for the killing.* He explained that William had no right under the law to forcefully resist Officer Albright in the performance of his duties during the traffic stop; and that is exactly what he did when he chose to push the officer's baton, which put in motion a series of events that resulted in the death of David Shermer.

"The People have proven each and every element of second degree murder beyond a reasonable doubt and it is your duty to find the defendant, William Thomas…"

(Taylor turned slowly and pointed to William, the image of the grim reaper extending his bony finger.)

"…Guilty of second degree murder."

"Ladies and Gentlemen, the life of a respected police officer, husband and father, has been needlessly snuffed out before his time. The evidence we have presented is clear and leads to only one reasonable and logical conclusion. The People have proven beyond a reasonable doubt that William Thomas is guilty of the murder of Officer Shermer, who was engaged, at the time of the murder, in the performance of his duties as a police officer. It is your duty to find him guilty and to find the special circumstance of murder of a peace officer. Thank you."

Now, get out there and win one for the gipper!

CHAPTER FORTY SIX

Brent walked up to the podium and set down his outline. This was his one and only chance to put everything together for the jury, which meant that he had to take apart everything that Benjamin Taylor had told them. He looked confident and together, in the same navy blue suit he had worn for his opening, like he was delivering the evening news.

"Ladies and gentlemen of the jury, good morning. When I told you that I disagreed with Mr. Taylor, and that this was a complicated case, I was both right and wrong. It *is* a complicated case, because none of the evidence points to a single, clear-cut conclusion. It is a simple case because to understand why it happened, all you have to do is look at the defendant, Mr. William Thomas."

Brent turned to look at William and then back at the jury. The jury seemed to Brent to be puzzled, but that is exactly what he wanted them to be.

"What went so wrong that night, the night that three guys returned home from a Dodger game, that caused the death of a police officer and the arrest of a respected lawyer? To understand that question, we need only to look at the color of William Thomas's skin."

"Objection, Your Honor," barked Taylor. "Irrelevant and highly prejudicial."

"Yes and no, Your Honor," Brent barked back. "Irrelevant? Hardly, but highly prejudicial? Yes, indeed."

"Overruled."

"When Officer Albright stopped William Thomas that night, in his mind he saw two niggers engaged in possible criminal activity, which was urinating in the bushes, and another nigger whom he assumed had been driving. Does that word make you uncomfortable?

Because, at one point in time, you have used it, or thought about using it?"

Brent searched the faces of the jury. They all appeared to be guilty of this societal misdemeanor. Every single one of them.

"What went wrong that night was something that went wrong in our society long ago that has never been corrected. Something that went wrong when a police officer assumes a black man is engaged in criminal activity for no other reason than he is a black man. Something that went wrong when a police officer assumed he could use deadly force on a black man during a drunk driving test just because he's black.

"You may think your job comes down to deciding who is telling the truth: John Albright or William Thomas. If you can't decide which version to believe, you must acquit William Thomas. But it goes far beyond that, ladies and gentlemen.

"Even if you believe John Albright and don't believe William Thomas, his two passengers, and Miss D., this is still not enough. The People have the burden to prove every element of this case beyond a reasonable doubt, which means that your feelings about what really happened cannot even come into play. What you *feel* about this must be completely ignored, as you must analyze whether the prosecution has proven every element of the case beyond a reasonable doubt. This, ladies and gentlemen, has not been done.

"First and foremost, Albright *never* saw William driving the car. He didn't exhibit any signs of being under the influence of alcohol, and passed the finger to nose test perfectly. Secondly, he had the right to defend himself when Albright shoved him with the baton because Albright's entire detention of William was illegal. Albright *knew* he wasn't under the influence of alcohol, and Albright had no reason to use bodily force when William had already been obeying his verbal commands.

"Secondly, even the prosecution's expert testified that it is impossible to determine from the fingerprints on the gun or the damage to the gun *who* actually fired it. And then you have two forensic experts. The People's expert says that it was Mr. Thomas who fired the gun, and the defense expert says it was John Albright. But, ladies and gentlemen, *it doesn't matter* who fired the gun.

"John Albright was the custodian of this gun. He is supposed to be the protector of the public, and only take it out when confronted with deadly force himself. The evidence clearly leads to only one conclusion, and that is that the death of

Officer Shermer was caused by John Albright, his partner. The very act of pulling out his gun was an exercise of excessive, deadly force which resulted in Shermer's death. William was already incapacitated. Albright was sitting on his chest when he pulled his gun. William wasn't going anywhere. He had no weapon with which to threaten Albright. There was no reason for Albright to draw his gun.

"This unreasonable use of deadly force put William's life in jeopardy, to the point where he legally had the right to defend himself with deadly force, if necessary. So you see, it was the act of pulling the gun out which caused the death of Officer Shermer. It doesn't matter whose finger was on the trigger because *the gun should not have been pointed at William's face in the first place!*" Brent said forcefully, as he slammed his fist on the podium.

Brent noticed several of the women unconsciously nodding at his argument. Now, time to reel in the men.

"Reasonable doubt tugs at every piece of evidence in this case. William, the designated driver, who had not had a drink, was suspected by Albright of driving under the influence of alcohol. This is not a crime for which deadly force should be used. *Period!* Officer John Albright was acting illegally when he used even bodily force to subdue William Thomas. Why didn't he radio for backup? Because he had a serious, unarmed drunk driver on his hands? It doesn't make any sense at all.

"Look at him! This is an innocent man!" Brent turned to William, who was choked with emotion, then back to the jury.

"You heard William testify that Officer Albright was going to erase him from the earth so his mother would not even recognize him at his funeral. You heard Mr. Washington and Mr. Jones say the same thing. You heard Miss D. testify that Albright had a propensity for violence and had also pulled his gun on an unarmed black prostitute when she had offended him and refused his advances.

"William thought he was going to be killed, and this perception is supported by the physical evidence. This belief that he was going to be killed, whether it was true or not, and that he was in grave physical danger with a gun pointed in his face, gave him the right to defend himself. And, as the judge will instruct you, if you are engaged in lawfully defending yourself and an innocent third party is killed, then you are not guilty because self-defense negates intent.

"Not only does self-defense negate intent in this case, it is a justifiable and legal excuse for homicide. Think about it. William is stopped by a zealous police officer who sees his black skin and immediately treats him like a criminal. How dare he refuse to be pushed around with a stick? A stick which the policeman uses to break his knee, several ribs, and puts him out cold on the pavement?

"Ladies and gentlemen, if William Thomas's skin had been white, this unfortunate event never would have happened. As the judge will instruct you, reasonable doubt is a fair doubt in your mind, which leaves you, after careful examination of all the evidence, in a state where you cannot say with an abiding conviction to a moral certainty that the particular element or charge against the defendant has been proven. If you find that any one element of the People's case has not been proven beyond a reasonable doubt, you must acquit William.

"The Judge will instruct you that, if there are two reasonable inferences you can draw from the evidence, one of which leads to the conclusion that he is guilty and one of which leads to the conclusion that he is *not* guilty, then you must select the inference that leads to the conclusion that he is not guilty.

"Did William get so enraged that he attacked a police officer who was shoving him with a club during a drunk driving test, or did the officer push the envelope too far when he shoved him with the baton? These are both inferences you can draw from the evidence and, under the law, you must choose the inference that the officer went too far when he used force that could inflict serious bodily injury.

"Think about it. William's got a concussion, six broken ribs, and a broken knee. Bruises and contusions all over. There's no evidence of *any* injuries of Officer Albright. Does that really sound like William got so violent and dangerous that Albright had to pull a gun on him to subdue him? It looks to me like William was the one who was in danger and had to worry about his life, not Albright.

"Did William wrench the gun away from Albright or push it away from his face? These are two different inferences that arise from the same evidence, and you have a legal obligation to choose the inference that he pushed it away from his face.

"Did William intend to gain control of the weapon and fire it to murder Albright or was he simply trying to save his own life? From the evidence, William was faced with having a gun in his face after having taken a beating, and Albright telling him that his mother would not recognize him at his funeral. Ladies and gentlemen, you must choose the inference that William was trying to save his own life.

"In fact, there is only one choice you have in this case, and that is to find William Thomas not guilty of the murder of David Shermer; because the prosecution has failed to prove every element of the crime beyond a reasonable doubt and because he had the right to defend himself from death or great bodily injury." Brent paused a beat, then said, "Thank you."

The silence of the courtroom turned to a buzz as reporters slipped away to make their reports and the other observers in the gallery began to whisper. Brent turned to William, who had tears in his eyes.

CHAPTER FORTY SEVEN

After the lunch break, the judge called the courtroom to order and invited Taylor to the podium to give his final closing remarks. Taylor again confidently hugged the sides of the lectern and regarded the jury.

"Ladies and gentlemen, George Orwell said that people sleep peacefully in their beds at night only because rough men stand ready to do violence on their behalf. This is a reality, and we have entrusted trained police officers to carry weapons to defend us from criminals. But in the process of defending themselves from criminals, they must also defend themselves.

"The defendant had no legal right to push away Officer Albright's baton, whether Officer

335

Albright was right or wrong in detaining him. It was the defendant's aggression toward Officer Albright's exercise of authority that caused the death of Officer Shermer.

"Mr. Marks says that there are two inferences that can both be drawn from the physical evidence. This is not true. The physical evidence clearly shows that Officer Albright's weapon had been tampered with. Officer Albright did not tamper with his own weapon. That could only have been the defendant. It was the defendant's refusal to yield to authority and the act of taking control over Officer Albright's gun which caused the death of David Shermer, an innocent party. If the defendant had succumbed to authority and stopped resisting, the situation would have never escalated to violence. That is the only reasonable conclusion you can draw from the evidence.

"Officer Albright had no choice but to draw his weapon. He had already been assaulted by the defendant, and was losing control over him. Drawing his gun was the only means of protection he had available to him at the time, as all other methods were on the other side of his duty belt and were unreachable.

"Were there other alternatives? This is something we cannot question. You are not allowed to use hindsight. Officers get killed in routine traffic stops. Officers get killed with their own weapons. When William Thomas put his hands on Officer Albright's weapon, he did two things: he broke the law, and he caused the death of Officer Shermer. *He knew* the potential deadly consequences of grabbing that weapon. *He knew* of the dangerous consequences to human life. Therefore, there can be no reasonable doubt that he is guilty of this crime."

Brent felt good about the case, but he also knew that anyone could be convicted of anything. Once the State decided to go after you (and they always did in cases where an officer of the law was killed), you were in peril. It was almost as if they didn't care what the outcome was. If the jury found William guilty, the system had done a good job of putting away a cop killer. If they found *for* William, the system had done a good job of identifying a bad cop. Either way, the State won. But it was not the same for Taylor. He had to win this one.

Judge Schwartz took center stage again, reading the jury instructions to the jurors. Some of them were taking notes, even though the jury instructions would be available for them to read in the jury room. Murder, reasonable doubt, and the presumption of innocence (which the judge and both lawyers had learned about in law school and on the job) were concepts that society expected the jury to get from this one-hour seminar on criminal law and defense. This was an exercise in idiocracy, but it had to be done. After the jury was sent off to the jury room to deliberate, the gallery cleared out completely. Brent shook William's hand before he was taken by the Bailiff, and he turned to Sarah and smiled. Sarah smiled back, knowing that William was innocent and that everything had been done that could possibly have been done to prove that. Taylor went out to talk to the reporters.

Brent stayed behind with Sarah. They would stay in the courtroom and wait for the verdict. He cautioned her that it is impossible to second guess a jury, but if they come back with a verdict right away, it's usually a not-guilty one. At five o'clock, the jury still had not spoken.

CHAPTER FORTY EIGHT

After two days of waiting, the court finally called Brent at his office. The jury had reached a verdict and he was due in court at 1:30 p.m. Brent called Sarah and flew out the door.

By the time Brent got to court, the doors had still not opened. Sarah arrived just in time as well. She threw her arms around Brent with emotion, and thanked him for helping. She was shaking.

The doors to Department N opened and Brent, Sarah, Taylor and a mob of reporters (as well as the curious public) filed in. William took his place at the counsel table with Brent. Judge Schwartz took the bench and the jury filed in, all wearing serious faces. Taylor, Brent and

William all stood up for them, although William felt like he was facing a firing squad.

"Ladies and gentlemen of the jury, have you elected a foreman?"

"We have, Your Honor," said George Fredericks, a retired postal worker.

"Mr. Foreman, have you reached a verdict?"

"Yes, Your Honor," said Fredericks.

"Please hand your verdict to the Clerk."

Fredericks handed the verdict over like it was something he was relieved to get rid of. The Clerk handed the verdict to the judge, who read it with absolutely no emotion. The seconds seemed to slow down during this entire process. The judge handed the verdict back to the Clerk.

"The Clerk will publish the verdict."

The Clerk stood, and William held his breath while Sarah prayed silently, although prayers could do nothing to change what had been written on that piece of paper at this point.

"We the jury, in the cause now pending before us, find the defendant, William Thomas, not guilty of murder."

William's knees buckled, and he braced himself from falling with his outstretched arms on the counsel table. Sarah cried. Taylor polled the jury. The verdict was unanimous.

"The Defendant, having been found not guilty, is discharged and is free to go after being processed," said the judge, who thanked the jury for their service. He absolved them of their duty of silence, except to keep quiet about the identity and testimony of Miss D, and told them they were welcome to speak to the attorneys. Taylor went into the corridor to speak with the several jurors who had stayed behind, but Brent stayed behind with Sarah to wait for William. He never spoke to juries and he didn't want to know how this one had come to their decision. It was often so nonsensical that he felt it was better never to know. All he did know was that justice, this time, had been done.

EPILOGUE

The sun was shining, the birds signing, and Danny and Sissy were running around in the back yard as William put the steaks on the grill. Jack relaxed and chatted with William and Brent as the steam rose from the barbeque and Angela sat with Sarah and watched the children play.

"There are no words I can say that can express to you two how thankful I am," said William. "I owe you my life."

"Just don't mess up my steak," said Brent.

William laughed, then asked, "What will happen to Albright?"

"He and his buddies will probably do time for running a prostitution ring. They've all been suspended from duty," said Jack.

"If only that solved the problem," said William.

"William, you're a part of the solution. Hopefully, your case will be a beacon for change and this country will finally stand for the principles that it says it believes in."

"I don't know about that, but at least one good thing came out of being in that jail."

"What's that?"

"You know that guy that I told you about who was protecting me in prison – Curly?"

"Yes, I remember. What about him?"

"Looks like he's in there on a bum rap himself. He's not a bad guy; just had to be tough to survive on the inside. I think I can get him out."

"That's how it works, William. One step at a time, one day at a time. It all begins and ends with us. All of us."

AFTERWORD

This is a fictional story, but it strikes at the heart of something which is tearing our country apart. We have become desensitized to violence and we have never been able to come to terms with our racist past. We have objectified people. We classify them and see them as objects instead of human beings. Our police forces are paramilitary forces that are in constant search of an enemy, and we have become too willing to accept war and violence as part of our existence as a country.

The prologue in this book is based on a true, real life story. The only difference is that the two boys were not black. If they had been, it could have been a completely different outcome.

This is not what this country is all about. This is not the country that I grew up in, where war was a bad thing and tolerance a good thing. We are a country of immigrants. We all belong here. The jury in the case depicted in this novel came to the right conclusion, but it could have just as easily gone the other way.

If we speak out against the abuses in our government and educate our children to be blind to skin color and tolerant of our neighbors, perhaps we can rise above our checkered past and we will not have to worry that the police will abuse their power.

Finally, I love to get email from my readers. Please feel free to send me one at info@kennetheade.com. I would also invite you to join my mailing list for advance notice of new books, free excerpts, free books, and updates. I will never spam you. Please subscribe here: http://bit.do/mailing-list.

One more thing...

I hope you have enjoyed this book, and I am thankful that you have spent the time to get to this point; which means that you must have received something from reading it. If you believe your friends would enjoy this book, I would be honored if you would post your thoughts and also leave a review on Amazon.

Best regards,

Kenneth Eade

info@kennetheade.com

BONUS OFFER

Sign up for paperback discounts, advance sale notifications of this and other books and free stuff by clicking here: http://bit.do/mailing-list. I will never spam you.

ABOUT THE AUTHOR

Author Kenneth Eade, best known for his legal and political thrillers, practiced law for 30 years before publishing his first novel, "An Involuntary Spy." Eade, an up-and-coming author in the legal thriller and courtroom drama genre, has been described by critics as "one of our strongest thriller writers on the scene, and the fact that he draws his stories from the contemporary philosophical landscape is very much to his credit." Critics have also said that "his novels will remind readers of John Grisham, proving that Kenneth Eade deserves to be on the same lists with the world's greatest thriller authors."

Says Eade of the comparisons: "John Grisham is famous for saying that sometimes he likes to wrap a good story around an important issue. In all of my novels, the story and the important issues are always present."

Eade is known to keep in touch with his readers, offering free gifts and discounts to all those who sign up at his web site, www.kennetheade.com.

CPSIA information can be obtained
at www.ICGtesting.com
Printed in the USA
LVOW01s1935010716
494942LV00014B/128/P